YULETIDE

A JANE AUSTEN-INSPIRED COLLECTION OF STORIES

ELIZABETH ADAMS   J. MARIE CROFT
AMY D'ORAZIO   LONA MANNING
ANNGELA SCHROEDER   JOANA STARNES
CAITLIN WILLIAMS

Edited by
CHRISTINA BOYD

quill ink

YULETIDE: A Jane Austen-inspired Collection of Stories

Copyright © 2018 by The Quill Ink

Cover and internal design © 2018 The Quill Ink, L.L.C.

Library of Congress Control Number: Cataloging-in-Publication Data

ISBN: 978-0-9986540-9-6

Cover design by Christina Boyd

Cover image by Under the Mistletoe, Making of America, 1873 (public domain)

Layout by Karen M Cox

PRAISE FOR THE AUTHORS

ELIZABETH ADAMS

Green Card, "You know the characters are interesting and well-crafted when four hundred pages doesn't feel like enough." —Austenesque Reviews

On Equal Ground, "This book marks her literary signature, she is not afraid to risk controversial stories and executes them beautifully!"— From Pemberley to Milton

The 26th of November, "I had a smile on my face the whole time I was reading this book. I sighed wistfully after finishing it and went back to my favorite scenes to enjoy it again." —Of Pens and Pages

CHRISTINA BOYD

The Darcy Monologues, "Think of *The Darcy Monologues* as your JAFF gateway drug. Don't worry, experts agree: it lowers anxiety, increases imagination, and is very good for health." —Period Drama Madness

Dangerous to Know: Jane Austen's Rakes & Gentlemen Rogues, "Each tells a story that was left out of Austen's original works. They manage to tell each in such a way it feels authentic to her vision and style." — Silver Petticoat Review

Rational Creatures, "...felt like slipping into the missing pages of Austen's own novels." —Drunk Austen

J. MARIE CROFT

Love at First Slight, "There was not a single thing I did not like about this novel. The author's sharp wit could rival that of Jane Austen...a pure delight to read." —Addicted to Austen

A Little Whimsical in His Civilities, "If there's an Austen hero that deserves a good chuckle at himself, I can think of none other more deserving than the proud and staid Mr. Darcy. Ms. Croft helps him loosen up his cravat in a manner that is playful, poetic and utterly romantic." —Just Jane 1813

AMY D'ORAZIO

The Best Part of Love, "...reels with intense drama and is so emotionally charged." —Readers' Favorite

A Short Period of Exquisite Felicity, "...a rollercoaster ride of emotions— angst, heartbreak, anger, then awe, shock, and love." —Of Pens and Pages

LONA MANNING

A Contrary Wind: A Variation on Mansfield Park, "Many try to emulate Austen; not all succeed. Here, Manning triumphs." —Blue Ink Review Starred Review

A Marriage of Attachment, "...wealth of historical events woven into this finely-tuned story line are seamless and enlightening." —Carole of Canada, Goodreads

ANNGELA SCHROEDER

The Goodness of Men, "Schroeder did an excellent job writing very tender, touching scenes between Elizabeth and Darcy (swoon!), and she added more depth to Darcy's backstory and the events that shaped him as the master of Pemberley." —Diary of an Eccentric

A Lie Universally Hidden, "Ms. Schroeder definitely knows how to pen some romantic and eloquent passages full of ardent yearning and devotion! *sigh*" —Austenesque Reviews

The Quest for Camelot, "This well researched book draws the reader into a story that immediately grabs the reader's interest so that one can't put it down until the end. And what an ending it is—full of surprises and romance." —Dr. Marty Turner, Amazon

JOANA STARNES

The Falmouth Connection, "Joana Starnes writes with great verve and affection about the familiar characters—and an intriguing cast of unfamiliar ones." —Jane Austen's Regency World Magazine

The Unthinkable Triangle, "...full of feeling...a book full of soul." — From Pemberley to Milton

Mr. Bennet's Dutiful Daughter, "'She did it again,' I told myself as I savored the feelings whirling around inside of me." —Just Jane 1813

CAITLIN WILLIAMS

Ardently, "To say I was swept away into the storyline may be an under-statement." —Just Jane 1813

The Coming of Age of Elizabeth Bennet, "This is a story to be completely and emotionally wrapped up in and consumed with!" —Austenesque Reviews

The Events at Branxbourne, "The evocative writing is of the highest quality and draws you in incompletely...flat out excellent." —Debbie B., Goodreads

TABLE OF CONTENTS

PRAISE FOR THE AUTHORS
DEDICATION

THE FORFEIT, Caitlin Williams...................................1
AND EVERMORE BE MERRY, Joana Starnes....................32
THE WISHING BALL, Amy D'Orazio.........................50
BY A LADY, Lona Manning...................................77
HOMESPUN FOR THE HOLIDAYS, J. Marie Croft..........101
THE SEASON FOR FRIENDLY MEETINGS,
Anngela Schroeder..137
MISTELTOE MISMANAGEMENT, Elizabeth Adams........153

ACKNOWLEDGMENTS, by the Editor, Christina Boyd

N.B. For authenticity, each author has written in the style and spelling pertaining to their story setting and era or proclivity to their prose. In the spirit of the collective and to be consistent throughout, this anthology adheres to US style and punctuation. Additionally, as a work inspired by Jane Austen's masterpieces, her own words and phrases may be found herein.

For friends of Jane Austen

THE FORFEIT

CAITLIN WILLIAMS

To be fond of dancing was a certain step to falling in love. —Jane Austen

She was almost home. Elizabeth Bennet was nearing the lane that led to Longbourn's front door and she longed to be warm again. Despite the thick snow that covered the fields surrounding Meryton, she had volunteered to take a note from her mother to Lady Lucas, reasoning that it was a short walk to Lucas Lodge, and the fresh air might restore her spirits.

Christmas festivities were rapidly overtaking Longbourn. Fires were lit in every room, the smell of baking pies permeated the air, and her small cousins—brought from Town by her uncle and aunt Gardiner a few days previously—were busy making decorations and noisily chasing each other about the house. It was usually her favourite time of year, when everyone was predisposed to laughter, love was limitless, and much joy was to be had from simple pleasures. She was generally a social creature and enjoyed all the parties and dinners along with the opportunities for dancing and music they afforded. This year, however, she was struggling to embrace the yuletide with the same delight.

Mostly because her elder sister was unhappy. Though she smiled and remained her affectionate, generous self, it was not difficult for

Elizabeth to see the hole that had been left in Jane's heart. Mr. Bingley had gone; Jane was deserted and bereft. Then there was Elizabeth's dear friend Charlotte Lucas's engagement to Mr. Collins, which made her both sad and a little angry at the world. Charlotte deserved a better life and a worthier companion than the pompous, ridiculous, obsequious, portly little man she had settled for.

In this reflective frame of mind, Elizabeth had walked to Lucas Lodge through a calm, picturesque, winter country scene. Yet after she had delivered her note, she had made the mistake of sitting with Charlotte for too long. When she chanced to look out the window, she saw that heavy snow had begun to fall atop the thick blanket which already covered the ground. Concerned that the lanes might become unpassable, she had immediately donned her outdoor clothes and hurried home.

Elizabeth knew every tree and hedgerow and could cut her way through them quickly, but she stopped abruptly just as Longbourn came within easy reach, taken aback by the curious sight of a carriage which had slid into a snowdrift.

She recognised the livery as Mr. Darcy's, and her astonishment was altogether complete when she realised Mr. Darcy, in his elegant great coat and tall hat, was pushing the carriage from behind with one of his servants while his driver and groom encouraged the horses from the fore. Their efforts were proving to be in vain; the carriage would not budge an inch.

She thought to go back and retrace her steps, to walk the long way around till she was at the back of the house where she might go in through the kitchen door. Detestable man that he was, she had no interest in exchanging pleasantries with Mr. Darcy. She deliberated for too long, however, giving Mr. Darcy the opportunity to look up and notice her.

He started in surprise but recovered quickly, bowed, and tipped his hat. "Miss Bennet."

"Mr. Darcy, I confess I never thought to see you in our small part of Hertfordshire again." Nor had she wanted to. She had said a private good riddance to the man less than a month ago when she had heard of his leaving for London after the Netherfield Ball.

"I have stopped only briefly on my way North. Mr. Bingley had a matter that needed personal attention at Netherfield. I merely came this way to be of assistance to him, and now I travel on to Matlock."

"Ah, but at this present moment, you appear to be travelling nowhere."

"A minor accident. We shall be away in a moment. The snow will stop shortly."

After a quick glance up at the sky, she gave him a doubtful look. "I should not count on it doing so merely because you have told it to, Mr. Darcy. The weather may prove less pliable than your friends."

His brow wrinkled as if he were confused. He stepped forward till he loomed over her, causing Elizabeth to remember what she had noticed the very first time they had met: he was decidedly masculine. None of his features were pretty, everything about him was dark—his hair and eyes were almost black. He was much taller than her, at least a foot, and his chest was broad. His shoulders were straight, his hands large and strong. Mr. Darcy had presence. Even when he was silent or ensconced in a corner, he was impossible to ignore.

She was conscious of her attraction to him. It rose up to vex her at their every encounter. He *looked* like the sort of a man she could lose her heart to—might be willing to entrust with her hand, even. It was fortunate she had quickly discovered he found her only tolerable. Otherwise she might have made a complete fool of herself over him and discovered his hateful character all too late. What worse tragedy could befall a girl than to be madly in love with a man before she discovered he was thoroughly detestable?

"The road North dips into a valley about a mile further up," she told him. "I should imagine it will be impossible to get through now, though I wish you the best of luck."

"I have excellent horses and a skilled driver in whom I have great faith. All will be well. Merry Christmas, Miss Bennet."

His "merry Christmas" was so sombre, so incongruous with the sentiment expressed that it made her smile. She wished him the same, offered him a small curtsey, and walked on.

They had not really exchanged the proper niceties; nobody had asked after anyone's health. Though perhaps that was a good thing. If she were to enquire after Mr. Bingley, she doubted she would be able to do so with any equanimity.

She had not gone ten feet, however, before she heard their resumed efforts to rescue the carriage come to naught. There was much heaving and mutterings of oaths, but it seemed firmly stuck.

Turning around, she raised her voice to be heard above the wind, which was now blowing in all directions, whipping snow up at her face. "Mr. Darcy, these roads and the surrounding terrain are as familiar to me as the lines on the palms of my hands. It would be foolhardy to continue. You will get no further North today and would do better to return to Netherfield."

"The house has not been readied," he shouted back. "I was there only for a few hours to conduct some business. I am certain there is not even a bed made up. I should not like to bother the staff."

"Would not a house, even one that is shut up, be better than freezing to death out on the road?"

Mr. Darcy glanced in the direction of Netherfield before a sudden gust of wind knocked him a step sideways. Elizabeth battled with it too and was fortunate to remain on her feet.

"You should not be concerned for my welfare, Miss Bennet. I ought to be concerned for yours and see you safely to your door."

"I am just a few moments away from safety. I beg you to take my advice and go back to Netherfield."

"Do you, Miss Bennet? I thank you for concern." He smiled, and she could not determine whether it was rendered strange because she had so rarely seen him smile or because he was staring at her so intently.

"I should worry for anyone who was attempting to travel in such weather. It is fast becoming a blizzard. You ought to make haste, whatever you decide."

At last he seemed to take notice of her warnings and glanced at the carriage and then at his men. One of them was not much more than a skinny boy who was shivering and stomping at the ground, clapping his hands together in an effort to keep warm.

"Unharness the horses, we will ride back to Netherfield and take shelter there," Mr. Darcy shouted. His groom quickly jumped to do his bidding.

Elizabeth tried to walk away, reasoning that he was a grown man with two other strapping men, a young lad, and some fine horses to assist him. After a few steps, though, she chastised herself. She ought to be charitable. It *was* Christmas, after all.

"Mr. Darcy," she said, hoping he could not tell she spoke through gritted teeth. "You are all wet and cold. At Longbourn you might dry off while your men can have something hot to eat and drink in the kitchen, and the horses might rest in the stables. Netherfield is three miles yonder, which is an easy distance in good weather but a thoroughly unpleasant one in this storm."

He shook his head proudly, but another strong gust of wind seemed to sap his resolve. His shoulders sagged. Though he did not deign to offer any thanks, he and his attendants began to follow her.

Mr. Darcy caught her up after a few moments, and she noticed him regard Longbourn suspiciously as they neared it, as if he were a lamb being led to the slaughter.

Perhaps her mother terrified him, Elizabeth mused. Having witnessed Mrs. Bennet's desperation and determination to see her daughters well wed, he might fear being trapped and held to ransom until he agreed to marry one of them. She shuddered. Being wed to Mr. Darcy was not a fate she should wish on any of them, no matter how much she sometimes despaired of Kitty and Lydia.

"Mr. Bingley could not come himself?" Elizabeth enquired, having to raise her voice to be heard over the wind.

"Oh, I suppose he might have, but I offered to spare him the trouble, as I would be passing nearby. He has no intention of returning to Netherfield in the near future and wished for me to speak to his steward."

"It would be better for the neighbourhood if he were to give it up altogether then, so we might see a new family settled there."

"I am glad we agree on this matter, Miss Bennet. Bingley and Netherfield were not a good match."

"It is difficult to settle in a new place, no matter how attractive a proposition it presents, if one's family and friends oppose it."

Mr. Darcy stopped and turned to face her. They were now only a few feet away from the house. "He would be foolish to disregard the feelings of those closest to him altogether. That would show a great deal of arrogance. A man must consider the duty he owes to his family before he makes any important decisions. Mr. Bingley took the lease of Netherfield on a whim, which is his way. He would do better to wait for an estate he might purchase outright—one that will complement his position in society or even enhance it."

Hateful man! Elizabeth fumed. She was quickly regretting her decision to extend a welcome to him. They were talking of Jane; he knew it as well as she did. "Perhaps he had an emotional attachment to the place," she said crossly, losing her composure. "He might have been exceedingly happy there if others had not made their displeasure so obvious."

"Yes, and no doubt he will see some other estate a few months hence that he becomes just as attached to. Netherfield is a good house but has some residual issues and difficulties attached to it."

Her temper was flaring, and who knows what she might have said next. Fortunately for her but unluckily for him, he was then hit directly on the nose by a large mound of snow. The attack was followed by some high-pitched giggling and a scurrying of boots in some nearby trees. Mr. Darcy looked both affronted and quite ridiculous as ice dripped from the end of his nose. He brushed it off with as much dignity as he could muster, while Elizabeth tried not to laugh. The snowball had most likely been thrown by her young cousin George, though she wished she had been brave enough to have launched it herself.

"Come on in now, George," she called out. "The weather grows worse and it is time for tea."

The butler, perhaps having heard voices from outside, opened the door. She quickly directed the man to show Mr. Darcy's servants where the stables and kitchen were and was relieved when Mr. Darcy went with them to see about his horses.

MOST OF THE family were gathered in the parlour and, once she had changed out of her boots, she joined them and was given a prized seat by the fire. When she told them of the invitation she had been forced to extend and to whom it had been extended, Kitty and Lydia both groaned while Mary congratulated on her Christian charity. Her father's and Mrs. Gardiner's eyebrows rose in interest, and her mother began a long speech detailing her dislike of the man.

Even through her thick boots, Elizabeth's stockings had gotten damp on her walk and her toes were cold. Comfortable in the familiarity of her family, she slipped off her shoes and rested her feet on the edge of the hearth.

Mr. Darcy took a long while to join them and walked in warily. However, he extended all the proper thanks and apologies, and he was polite when introduced to those he did not already know. Elizabeth watched him carefully as he greeted her uncle and aunt. To her surprise, he did not recoil in disgust and instead shook hands courteously with Mr. Gardiner, even going so far as to ask after his line of business.

When he took a chair, though, he retreated to a corner of the room and seemed content to be overlooked as the conversation began again and went on around him.

"Lizzy," Jane whispered into her ear, making her start. When Elizabeth looked at her sister, Jane nodded at her feet. Realising her stockings were on show and that her skirts had ridden up to almost her calves, she straightened in her chair and slipped her shoes back on. Mr. Darcy, when she glanced over at him, was looking at the hearth at the exact spot where she had been warming her toes. He seemed to be deep in thought before his head rose to meet her gaze, and colour flooded his cheeks. Elizabeth moved to find a seat a little further away from the fire. A half hour before, she had been chilled down to the bone; now she felt very hot indeed.

HE WAS to stay for dinner, of course, for the storm showed no signs of abating. His promised presence at the table caused a great deal of furious whispering amongst the Bennet girls as they descended the stairs after dressing. It was eventually decided by Lydia that it was

Elizabeth's duty to take the seat next to him. It was somehow her fault that the "dreadful bore that no one cared a fig for" was stranded amongst them.

"What would you have her do, Lydia?" Jane whispered softly. "She could hardly leave him struggling to free his carriage until the cold had turned him to stone."

"No, I could not," Elizabeth sighed. "Though I wonder if anyone would notice any difference."

It made all of them laugh but Jane, who tried, yet failed to bring them to order. They burst upon the drawing room, colourful and loud. Mr. Darcy flinched. They were, Elizabeth suspected, too much of an assault upon his senses.

He was an almost silent dinner partner, though he ate heartily and, before the ladies rose to leave the men to their port, he thanked Mrs. Bennet most sincerely for the meal and complimented her on it most elegantly.

Their mother, who was always as eager for praise as she was for news of single young gentlemen in the neighbourhood, softened with alarming fickleness under his words. Once the ladies were alone with their sewing, she began expounding on his qualities and manners with as much energy as she had decried them earlier. Elizabeth was left musing upon the beneficial effect a few kind words could have. It was a shame that some people did not exert themselves to be so generous more often.

SLEEP DID NOT COME EASILY. How could it when her tormenter lay in a bed just down the corridor? The thought caused her to toss and turn until the early hours of the morning. When her fretful mind did finally allow her some rest, she had the oddest, most disturbing of dreams.

Thankfully, he was absent at breakfast, having gone out early and taken his own men and every able-bodied man at Longbourn to recover his carriage except for her papa, who had claimed himself busy and retreated to his library. Elizabeth expected her father would remain there for the best part of the day and felt like following him.

They would likely be confined to the house for the foreseeable future, and spending the day engrossed within the pages of a good book seemed a capital plan.

She lingered over her toast and pushed her eggs around her plate listlessly. When she saw Mr. Darcy trudging back up the front path, a furious expression on his face and his hat in his hand, she swallowed the last of her tea quickly and decided to make good her escape. She was choosing a book when she heard some colourful language being used beyond the library window. Both she and Mr. Bennet looked out to see Mr. Darcy throw his hat upon the snow and then kick it across the park in frustration.

Mr. Bennet chuckled. "It was cold enough to give the devil a chill last night. Even if he extracts his carriage, the roads will be frozen solid. The ice will prove too treacherous for his horses, as he knows only too well. Mr. Darcy, I suspect, will be our guest this Christmas, Lizzy. How ever shall we amuse him?"

ELIZABETH HAD ONCE HEARD Mr. Bingley remark that he did not know of a *"more awful object than Darcy, on particular occasions, in particular places; at his own house especially, and of a Sunday evening when he has nothing to do."*

Not that she had any respect for Mr. Bingley's judgement of late, but in this he was proved correct. Mr. Darcy, constrained and imprisoned by the snow, had become a brooding, restless creature who frightened small children. Upon seeing him enter the drawing room, her cousins would hide under tables or scamper from the room.

Though she could not very well take refuge beneath the furniture, Elizabeth tended to follow their example. She ran from Mr. Darcy whenever the opportunity of escape presented itself.

The man had trouble sitting still. He roamed Longbourn's corridors while scowling at his watch. He would examine the skies through every window he passed, perhaps hoping the next might offer a view that showed particular signs of a thaw that the window three feet away which he had looked out moments before did not.

Clearly, he liked occupation, to be always doing something, and presently he had nothing to expend his energy on. It was as if he were a spring, being wound tighter and tighter by his imprisonment. Jane, with her soft smiles and calm manner, managed to soothe him somewhat, and he amazed Elizabeth by seeking her sister out when even he seemed to be irritated by his own pacing. He would sit beside her while she sewed, offering the occasional comment, asking the odd question, but generally, he was silent.

Her father tried to ply him with port in an effort to put at him ease, only to discover he was not much of a drinker.

Her mother tried to ply him with food, but there were only so many puddings and pies a man could eat in one day without feeling ill.

It was Mrs. Gardiner who eventually managed to draw him out, to exchange with him just enough words as might legally constitute a conversation.

They were sat in the drawing room in the late afternoon while most of the family were engaged in a game of cards with the exception of Elizabeth, her aunt, and Mr. Darcy. He was supposedly reading, but his book did not seem to hold his attention, for he shifted in his seat and frequently gave a heavy sigh.

"It is a shame you will not have Christmas at Pemberley, Mr. Darcy. Such a beautiful house, and how pretty the grounds would be, all covered in snow," Mrs. Gardiner said.

"You have seen Pemberley, Mrs. Gardiner?" he asked, immediately shutting his book without bothering to mark his place.

"Oh yes, Mr. Darcy. I grew up in Lambton, not five miles from Pemberley." She smiled at him before modestly informing him that he would not remember her family, for they would have moved in very different circles.

Elizabeth half expected him to sniff and open his book again, but he grew animated and there followed a long exchange with her aunt. Elizabeth had never seen him so lively as he spoke of horse chestnut trees, smithies, tors, rivers, and beauty spots they both knew.

"I dearly love the countryside around Pemberley, Mrs. Gardiner, but I was not headed there. We have not had Christmas at Pemberley since my mother died. She had methods of making it special. She would hide presents around the house for me to find. Ridiculous gifts, silly things such as a pine cone, a bag of dried fruit, or a handkerchief. I gained far more enjoyment from searching out those small presents than I did any expensive item from my father. Since her passing, my sister and I have joined our family at Matlock almost every year. While we have a pleasant time, it has never been quite the same. Another family's customs and traditions can never mean as much as your own."

This speech made Elizabeth oddly emotional—she had no idea of when Mr. Darcy's mother had died or what the family at Matlock were like—but her imagination conjured up an image of a happy young boy running around a grandiose house looking for trinkets one year, then walking mournfully around, his hat draped in black crepe the next. She saw him being driven from his home to spend Christmas with austere relatives, his baby sister opposite him in the carriage on a nurse's knee; the baby blissfully unaware but the boy desperately missing his mother.

She had a sudden urge to go and kiss her own mother, a feeling which, she shamefully acknowledged, rarely overcame her, and she managed to easily resist it.

Instead she got to her feet. "One of our customs, Mr. Darcy," she said, clapping her hands to gain everyone's attention, "when Christmas draws so near, is the singing of carols. We have been neglecting our traditions, and that must be remedied."

Mary, as eager as she always was to display her questionable skills, made a dash towards the pianoforte. Elizabeth was lighter on her feet, however, and beat her to the stool, where she sat down triumphantly. Mary sulked while everyone else seemed relieved. When Elizabeth began to play, the mood of the room lifted. They laughed at each other when they went wrong, applauded Mr. Gardiner's perfect baritone on the lower notes, and managed some true harmony, not always in their song, but in their sentiments and feelings.

Mr. Darcy was urged forward to join them several times but declined. He moved to the card table, where her nephews, who did not enjoy the singing, were busy trying to make a pyramid out of cards. Taking a seat between them, he began to assist.

By the time the carols had made the singers all thirsty and they stopped to refresh themselves, the tower was several stories high, and Mr. Darcy did not look quite so foreboding as he had previously. His shoulders had been almost as high as his ears, but now his posture was loose. He smiled when she came near him, stopped her to tell her how much he had enjoyed the music. His unspent energy, the frustration which had looked fit to consume him, appeared to have dissipated.

What had caused the change, she could not say—Mrs. Gardiner's speaking of Pemberley, his time with the children, the carols perhaps? Whatever it was that was making him more amiable by the minute, she could only be glad of it, and she was pleased his congenial mood carried over into the morning.

When Elizabeth nonchalantly mentioned during breakfast that she had liked his mother's idea of a Christmas treasure hunt and how the Gardiner children might enjoy such an activity—confined to the house as they were—he immediately jumped up, found paper and pen and started planning one for them.

Caught up in the excitement, Elizabeth worked alongside him at every turn. They hid treasures and made maps together at a table; their elbows bumping as frequently as their intellects while they turned phrases over and thought up clues. They sat next to each other at the top of the stairs when the hunt commenced, enjoying the excitement they had created and smiling at each other as George held the chubby hand of his smallest sister, helping her along rather than selfishly dashing off to seek his own prizes.

"I am willing to forgive the snowball incident," Mr. Darcy said. "He is an excellent boy."

Elizabeth could only smile; she was unusually lost for words. He was as much of a puzzle to her as the game they had created for the children—who were now more inclined to run after him rather than away from him. They would tug at his coattails and call his name, beg him to swing them around—and he would put aside his dignity and do so, no matter how many times they asked.

Was this really Mr. Darcy? The same despicable Mr. Darcy whose officious interference had ruined Jane's chances of happiness with Mr. Bingley? The same Mr. Darcy who had acted so dishonourably towards Mr. Wickham? She realised with a jolt that she had rarely thought of Wickham in the last few days.

Then he was there! Mr. Wickham himself, along with two or three other officers, at the front door of Longbourn. As there had been no callers for three days, their arrival was greeted with astonishment. Shrieks of laughter and delight were heard from Kitty and Lydia, who ran out into the cold to greet them. When Elizabeth went to the door, she saw they had acquired a sledge from somewhere and had attached to it two great shire horses.

They looked delighted by their own ingenuity and were showing off, standing atop the sleigh while declaring that nothing could keep them from calling upon their favourite ladies. Wickham, Elizabeth was glad to note, was more circumspect, not so loud or bragging, and came towards her with a sheepish smile. He bowed gallantly and apologised for his companions' boisterousness.

"Though I own I was equally eager to call, as I …." He stopped mid-sentence as something over her shoulder caused a look of fear to cross his countenance. "Darcy. You are the last person I expected to see."

"And the last one you wanted to, I imagine," Mr. Darcy replied from behind her. "Might we speak in private, Wickham?"

Though she remained with Kitty and Lydia—determined to ensure they did not lose all sense of propriety—Elizabeth managed to observe Mr. Darcy and Mr. Wickham talking in a far corner of the hall. She could not hear what was said, for it was all carried on in hushed tones, but it looked very much like Wickham was receiving a lecture.

When he came into the room to join the rest of the party, Mr. Wickham took a seat next to her. He rolled his eyes and leaned towards her, whispering, making her his conspirator.

"Not content with having stolen everything from me, he sees fit to play the role of my lord and master. How I abhor the rich and the power they wield over us! I confess I would be happy with fifty pounds a year, a small piece of land I might call my own, and a few chickens and geese to roam upon it. Yes, how content I would be then, as long as God granted me a beautiful partner in it all. Someone with whom I could share my interests and passions, someone who understood me."

He smiled at her softly. "Do you deplore me for not telling Darcy off, for not standing up to him as I ought? You see, I still cling to the hope he might gain a conscience and reward me with something, as his father would have wished him to."

She made no reply but found herself wanting to move away. Previously, she had enjoyed their talks, the easy intimacy that existed between them. His flirting, his manners, everything had pleased her immensely. Yet now, for a reason she could not quite determine, she was uncertain of him.

"Do you know he had the temerity to warn me off you? I am apparently banned from going within ten feet of a Bennet girl! Shall we pretend to be madly in love to spite him, Miss Elizabeth?"

"I am afraid I am not adept at acting, Mr. Wickham," she replied. "Is it something at which you excel?"

He blinked and appeared alarmed, could not look at her for a few moments. "Please tell me he has not turned you against me as he has the rest of the world? I could not bear that. You must know I have hopes, hopes I cannot yet voice."

He was so handsome, his voice so lyrical, and his manners so good that it was difficult not to feel flattered by his addresses. "I am not against you," she replied quickly. "Yet I must tell you that on becoming further acquainted with Mr. Darcy, I feel I may have been unfair. Not that I forgive his trespasses against you, but I do believe I begin to understand his disposition better. I cannot quite hate him as I once did. There is a certain kindness about him which is incongruous with some of his past behaviour."

"As I have said before, he can be liberal and generous when he chooses to be," Wickham said blithely. His attention was then caught by the general conversation that was occurring on the other side of the room, and he turned away from her to better hear it.

Elizabeth only half listened, as she was busy watching Mr. Darcy enter the room. The frown that had been missing all day had returned to his countenance. *Why did he have to be so dour?*

"She has ten thousand pounds left to her by an uncle. I wish someone would die and leave me ten thousand pounds," Lydia cried, leaving Elizabeth thoroughly ashamed of her. She thought to quiet her, but Lydia went on before she could intervene. "All the men will want to dance with her and will want to kiss and romance her, but they will not mean it, for she is such a nasty little freckled thing. No one could truly admire her."

Wickham laughed at Lydia's speech. "Who do you speak of?"

"Mary King, of course," Lydia announced. "Wait till you see her, Wickham. She is not very pretty. Oh, what a shame Colonel Forster's party on Christmas Eve will not be possible."

"The party is to go ahead," one of the officers said. "Have you not heard? The house he has taken is so conveniently situated in the centre of Meryton that a great number of the guests can walk to it."

Kitty pouted. "We cannot walk."

"Then we shall send the sleigh for you, and you will be conveyed home on it afterwards," Wickham declared, to the delight of almost the entire room. Mr. Darcy's frown grew deeper.

Elizabeth interjected that her parents might object to the plan, but no sooner had she given voice to the caution than Mrs. Bennet entered. Upon being told of the scheme, she squealed as loudly as Lydia had. Mr. Bennet would agree to almost anything if it meant his wife would leave him in peace, and so it seemed they were to go.

"You will not join us I suppose, Darcy?" Wickham asked. "Music, dancing, levity, and conversation. Not your favourite pastimes, are they?"

"On the contrary, if the invitation extends to me, I shall be there," Mr. Darcy replied, before rising from his seat, bowing to the room and leaving them.

THEIR VISITORS REMAINED LESS than an hour. The days were short, and darkness was falling rapidly. As soon as they had been waved off, Elizabeth found her warmest coat and hat and decided to risk a short stroll in the shrubbery, the paths of which had been partially cleared. It was still freezing, cold enough to rob her of her breath, but she could bear ten minutes without if it meant some fresh air. The layers of snow made everything still and quiet, and so she heard Mr. Darcy's approach long before she saw him.

After a remark on the beauty of the scene, with which she concurred, he walked a few feet away as if he were about to go on without her, but then changed his mind, turned, and stopped. "It is no business of mine, but may I take the liberty of cautioning you against Mr. Wickham? I have heard your sisters tease you about him, and he does *appear* to favour you, but I should not count on his attentions lasting. You are too poor, I am afraid, to be a serious object with him."

Her mouth hung open in shock at his bluntness.

"Money is his motivation in all things, Miss Bennet," Mr. Darcy continued, moving closer to her. "I hope you will not feel too wounded when he transfers his affections elsewhere."

"Mr. Darcy, to have reduced him to his current state is crime enough, must you seek to slander him too? He has not the means at present to think of a future with any lady, but that may not always be the case, and he is not fickle. He is most loyal to the memory of your father, which is why he will not publicly expose you."

"His curious way of not exposing me, Miss Bennet, is to relate his story of my supposed misdeeds to everyone he meets."

Her temper, which has been in full flow, suddenly had the wind knocked out of its sails. For he was right! Mr. Darcy had made it easier for the residents of Meryton to dislike him by standing about disdainfully at every gathering, but it was Mr. Wickham's tales that had truly confirmed him as a villain in everyone's eyes. Wickham had not been discreet, not at all.

"Who is this girl with the ten thousand pounds?" Mr. Darcy asked.

"Mary King."

"Miss Bennet, I have no doubt you will look exceedingly pretty tomorrow night. You will be as charming and witty as ever. You will dance or sing or play beautifully, yet Mr. Wickham will not single you out. He will not spare a thought for your feelings or feel the slightest guilt when he transfers his attentions from you to Miss King. He is without conscience."

"I think you are wrong, Mr. Darcy," she said but, truthfully, she felt less sure of herself with every passing moment. "Perhaps you try to lessen the effect of your own crimes against him by sabotaging his character."

"Shall we have a wager on it?"

"For money?" she exclaimed.

"Oh, no. I would not take money from a lady. If I am wrong, I will pay you a forfeit, and if you are wrong, then I will extract a forfeit from you."

"Do I get to choose the forfeit?" she asked warily.

"Why not? Please, go ahead."

"Very well. If Mr. Wickham does not single Mary King out tomorrow night, you will write a letter to Mr. Bingley. In it, you will inform him that my sister will be in Town after Christmas, staying with my uncle, and you are certain she would welcome a call from him."

Mr. Darcy was smug. "If I am wrong, Miss Bennet, I will go to Town myself for the express purpose of encouraging the call."

"And you will withdraw your opposition to my sister? You will not interfere between them at all? It is no use denying it, Mr. Darcy, I know that you have."

"I will not deny it, yet I do regret it."

Her head snapped up in surprise. "You do?"

"I have heard your mother previously, Miss Bennet, talking about my friend Bingley as if he were nothing more than a walking, talking pound note. I wrongly assumed your sister regarded him in the same manner." He sighed and leant on his stick. "I did not imagine his leaving would cause her any great pain. I now see that it has. I will gladly pay my forfeit if I lose, but I will not lose."

Elizabeth nodded in satisfaction. "I am certain that I will not either, so it hardly matters but, out of interest, what is to be my forfeit?

"Oh, I have not decided yet." He straightened up and began to walk away. "I shall let you know when I do. Enjoy your walk, Miss Bennet," he called over his shoulder.

Diverting from the paths, kicking up snow and making her petti-coats wet, Elizabeth spent longer outside than she had first intended. She needed time to think through all he had told her—about Wickham, about Bingley—and about that which most perturbed her. Somewhere, during their odd exchange, had he really described her as witty, charming, and pretty?

It took very little to excite Kitty's and Lydia's sensibilities and, as they sat down to breakfast on Christmas Eve, they did so with the prospect of dancing with handsome men in red coats, of escaping Longbourn for a few hours, and of a sleigh ride. It was too much to expect any decorum. They could barely sit still, and their feverish anticipation of it all was only bound to increase as the day went on.

Elizabeth shuddered to think of how it would be: endless giggling over nothing, shouting and running about, in and out of bedrooms with arms full of skirts, stealing ribbons, gloves and jewellery as they went. For her two younger sisters, the process of getting dressed to attend Colonel Forster's party was likely to last longer than the party itself. They talked over one another at the table, argued about which of the officers was most handsome, and they mocked Mary when she declared such pleasures puerile and insisted that they would do better to remain at home in order to "strengthen their intellects by reading."

Mr. Darcy had taken up a newspaper as soon as he had finished eating, his face hidden for some time. Elizabeth thought—in fact she had prayed—that he had not been paying much attention to Kitty and Lydia's nonsense, but now he lowered the pages to look in Mary's direction. "I see you and I share a similar turn of mind, Miss Mary. Perhaps we ought to form an alliance this evening to protect ourselves from the evils of too much merriment. If we must dance, and I fear it will be demanded of us, perhaps we might stand up together and discuss something valuable and sensible while we go through our steps? Will you do me the honour of the first dance?"

The table fell silent and all eyes turned to Mary, who blushed furiously but nodded her acceptance. She thanked him in a voice so small and high-pitched it was in danger of shattering the water glasses, then excused herself and almost ran from the room.

All was still for a few moments, though Elizabeth detected a slight shaking in her father's shoulders as if he were trying to hold in a laugh.

"So, are you going to dance with all of us, Mr. Darcy?" Lydia asked. "Or stand about stupidly like you did when we first met you?"

Both Elizabeth and Jane opened their mouths to admonish her, but Mr. Bennet was quicker, and his dressing down was surprisingly efficient and effective—so much so that Lydia spent the rest of the meal with her head cowed over her plate.

Mr. Darcy seemed thoughtful as he finished the last of his coffee and declined another cup, telling them he intended to walk to the turnpike to assess the state of the roads.

After he had left the room, Mrs. Bennet whispered furiously at Mr. Bennet, telling him she thought Mr. Darcy might be in love with Mary. In reply, their father rolled his eyes and looked as if he could not decide who was more ridiculous: his wife, or himself for having married her.

Elizabeth passed Mr. Darcy in the hall just as he was preparing to go out. "I suppose you go to the turnpike to see whether it would be prudent to travel yet. I cannot blame you for wanting to flee."

He shook his head. "I require the exercise—and six ladies readying themselves for an evening party! I know enough of such things to realise I would be an annoyance and in everyone's way if I were to remain."

"'Tis true. It takes a great deal of preparation and fuss for some of us Bennets to make ourselves *tolerable* enough to appear in company."

He put a hand to his chest and bowed. "A hit, madam. Well deserved."

"I am a little unfair." She smiled, and he looked at her for a long moment with an odd expression in his eyes that she could not quite fathom. "My apologies, Mr. Darcy.

"No, do not apologise. You must allow me to make some reparation for that ill-judged, hasty remark, else I fear I may never be allowed to forget it. Let me say that in your case, Miss Bennet, no preparations are necessary." He reddened, started to say something more but then seemed to change his mind. "Your smiles give you an unfair advantage in our wager. If I did not know Wickham so well, I might be more worried about losing."

She coloured herself, recognising his awkwardness. He was not used to giving compliments; they did not come lightly or easily to him as they did other gentlemen. It took a moment for her to recover. "You are not backing out of our agreement are you, Mr. Darcy?"

"Not at all, madam." He stuck out his hand. "We did not shake on it before. Let us do so now."

She put her hand into his without thinking. Neither wore gloves; his were still hanging out of his coat pocket. The contact was not fleeting, and he clasped her fingers for longer than was polite or necessary. The feelings his touch generated did not shock her. Of course, she should feel hot and overcome! Something oddly familiar, yet thoroughly exciting, coursed through her veins, but then, he was a handsome man; the sensations were natural. Strangely, she was both relieved and disappointed when he let go, bowed his head, and walked quickly to the door.

Once he had gone, she ran up the stairs to immediately choose a gown, then ran down again with it in her arms to see about getting it pressed. She bothered the busy upstairs maid to discuss how they might later style her hair and went to ask Jane if she might borrow a particular pair of earrings. Then she called for a bath. It was only when she was sunk deep into the iron tub that she realised she had spent the last two hours in much the same fashion as Lydia and Kitty, minus, thankfully, some very silly giggling.

It was dark when the sleigh arrived to collect them. Mr. Darcy went out first, a lantern in his hand, to inspect it closely. He frowned a great deal but at last declared it safe and, when it had been loaded with hot bricks from the fire and many rugs, they were all allowed to climb into it. He did not appear to trust the driver, however, and made the man move over on the front bench.

Taking up the ribbons himself, he gave them an elegant flick, clicked his tongue, and the horses moved forwards. They all gave a gasp of delight as they were driven out of the park and into the surrounding lanes towards Meryton.

Elizabeth turned her face up towards the sky. The moon was bright and the stars shone down upon them, guiding their way. She listened to the scraping noise made by the sleigh's runners as they moved over the ice and knew she would always remember this journey, even when she was grey and old. Perfect wintry night skies and that particular sound would forever remind her of this moment.

Sadly, the beauty of it all was soon eclipsed by Lydia's whining.

"We are going very slowly, Mr. Darcy. All the officers will be already engaged for the first dance by the time we arrive."

"Shush, Lydia," Mrs Bennet said. "I am sure he is being careful for Mary's sake. I am certain he would not want any harm to come to her."

COLONEL FORSTER'S party could not be described as a ball as such, but everybody had arrived inclined to dance. The Bennets burst upon the scene just as the musicians were about to begin. They all went in hurriedly, to be greeted by their friends and neighbours, who exclaimed with pleasure as if they had not seen them for months rather than mere days.

The efforts they had expended in simply getting there made everyone determined to enjoy themselves. The room was not big and they were rather tightly packed into it, but it was prettily decorated with bunches of holly and garlands made from ferns and berries.

Mr. Wickham, upon seeing Elizabeth, immediately came forward and asked her for the first dance. She readily acquiesced and, when they took their place in the set, she could not help but look down the rows of couples for Mr. Darcy, who was stood opposite Mary. Their eyes met, and she gave him a smile she hoped was as smug as the one he had worn the day before. He only nodded at her in return.

Her triumph, however, was short-lived. They had not been dancing more than five minutes before Wickham asked her to point out Mary King to him. He laughed when she did and pretended no interest, but neither did he seem to care for anything else Elizabeth had to say. His eyes frequently wandered in Miss King's direction.

"What do you think, Mr. Wickham? Is she 'a nasty freckled thing' as Lydia has described her?"

"Your sister is too harsh whereas I, as a gentleman, am not. I am certain the young lady has many attractive qualities."

"Oh, yes," Elizabeth replied. "Ten thousand of them." She tried to smile as if it were a joke, but she was disappointed in him and her tone was harsher than she intended.

He was taken aback but only laughed before returning to his usual ways with her. They flirted and joked, yet Elizabeth did not do so with any honesty. Instead, it became a courtly game, one that must be played out until they reached the end of their half hour together. Elizabeth was relieved when he did not linger with her at the end of the dance.

Wickham joined the throng of officers who were vying to stand up with Mary King. As charming and as handsome as he was, Elizabeth strongly suspected he would prove victorious. As she stood by her mother, she saw him work his way stealthily to the lady's side, then hold out his hand. He made his request with a wolfish smile and was readily accepted.

Mr. Darcy, likewise, had a new partner and was leading Jane across the room to dance. After this, he asked Kitty, and then Lydia. Elizabeth was dancing herself and most likely annoying her partner by almost never looking his way. Yet how could she when the horrifying spectacle of Lydia and Mr. Darcy dancing was so near? So mismatched were they, such opposites in every respect, that they were uncomfortable to watch. Even so, she could not stop staring at them.

Upon re-joining her friends, Elizabeth took a deep breath and straightened the sash on her dress. He would come now, she thought, if he was really to dance with them all. It was surely her turn to be asked and Mr. Darcy did take a step her way but, before he was even halfway across the room, a Lucas son, home from Cambridge for Christmas, tapped her on the shoulder and requested the honour. She could hardly refuse and let herself be led away, only to look over her shoulder and see Mr. Darcy approach Charlotte.

Would he never sit down? Could he not stand on the side and look them all over critically as he was once wont to do? Why did she feel so aggrieved, so full of rage? Was this *jealousy* she felt? How silly to be envious of Charlotte, who had already made her somewhat dubious choice of mate! Yet the set ought to have been hers—it was her turn to dance with Mr. Darcy.

How many dances were left? Not many, she feared. They had taken supper already, and this gathering could not last much longer. The guests would have to consider travelling home in the inclement weather. Some of the older ladies would take an early leave, and their sons, daughters, and husbands would go with them.

Added to the problem of the snow, some of the officers were growing rowdy. Colonel Forster had recently ordered one of his men—who had looked quite green in the face—to bed. If they continued to drink, they would soon become unfit for the company of ladies; all those with reputations to consider would withdraw and leave the men to their own kind of revelry.

Elizabeth's despair grew greater when Mr. Darcy decided upon Mary King for his next partner. Her mother, standing next to her, was equally disappointed. "Oh, he has only danced with our Mary once, and now he chooses Miss King. I begin to doubt his admiration."

"I begin to doubt everything, even myself," Elizabeth replied, before being approached by a stout, young officer. She gave her hand to him with a sigh.

As she had predicted, for some of gathered families, the end of the next set was the end of the night. The Lucases departed, along with a few others, giving their "merry Christmases" and wishes for a safe journey home.

The officers were keen to keep the dancing alive, however. One of them climbed upon the shoulders of another and was given a great cheer when he hung a small sprig of mistletoe from a beam.

Elizabeth knew what was to follow. This was the country, not a formal gathering in Town. There would be a reel or a jig, something fast, and at the end of it, as the couples took their final steps down the line, the lady would bestow a kiss on the cheek of her partner. A harmless Christmas ritual in Meryton, probably not the thing at

Matlock or Pemberley. Yet when Mr. Darcy came near, she could not breathe for wondering what he would say or do.

All he did, however, was to tug at his cuffs and stare at the scene before him. Partners were being selected—more carefully than ever before, as gentlemen sought out their favourites.

"You may want to look away, Mr. Darcy. I have no doubt you will heartily disapprove of what is to follow."

"I suppose the entertainment being what it is, you will win our wager. Your faithful Mr. Wickham will no doubt be along in a moment to ask you to dance."

The moment he had finished speaking, Mr. Wickham did step in their direction. Elizabeth's heart stopped briefly. Then he smiled tightly, almost apologetically at her, before approaching Mary King with sickeningly false humility and a pretence of shyness.

"Congratulations, Mr. Darcy. You win," she said, leaving him to go over to a chair in the corner. She sank into it with an air of defeat.

"I have won nothing."

She looked up to see he had followed her. He glanced around the room before crouching down beside her chair. "You are much better rid of him. I pity the poor lady he does marry. His tale—of the living he was supposed to have? What he always neglects to omit is that, after my father died, he declared he never wanted to take orders. Instead, he asked for financial recompense. I gave him a large sum of money, which he has now most likely squandered."

His voice dropped to a mere whisper. "One day when we are alone, I will tell you of another wrong he did me which I have had to keep secret for the sake of someone who is very dear to me."

"I am thoroughly ashamed of my own lack of judgement. How could I be fooled so easily?"

Mr. Darcy sighed. "My father was a great and truly wise man. Yet, to his last breath, he adored that scoundrel. I myself was friends with Wickham for many a year before I saw just how despicable he can be. Do not blame yourself and do not hide in a corner. This is no place for you. Come along."

She did not give him her hand; he took it from her lap, and she followed him silently to the dance, which had already begun. He

24

pulled her into the throng of whirring couples. Normally an excellent dancer, she was so surprised by the quickness of his step that she stumbled. He was forced to put his hand on her waist briefly to steady her.

"You must try and keep up with me, Miss Elizabeth."

She laughed. "I thought you did not like to dance, Mr. Darcy?"

"I do not generally. Though any chore is made easier and more enjoyable when there is the promise of a reward at the end of it."

Speech was thus rendered impossible; *looking* at him was rendered impossible. It was all she could do to put her feet where they ought to go. The room grew hotter, the dance faster. Everything else fell away: the loud, colourful room, the other couples turning as furiously, the noise of a dozen shoes on the floorboards, the laughter. All she could think of was that they were coming to the end. They were moving down the set, the mistletoe looming ever nearer. There was applause and louder laughter as the first kiss was bestowed, and then another, and then another. Of course, she would do the same. She would kiss his cheek. It *was* Christmas, after all. When they were finally under that little sprig of greenery, she stood on the tips of her toes to reach him, expecting him to offer his cheek.

Instead he quickly caught her face between his hands and kissed her, properly, fully on the mouth. His lips felt firm and tasted sweet, and that was all she was conscious of before he let her go, and then mortification took hold of her.

The laughter that followed their encounter was louder than ever, the applause even stronger. Knowing it would be worse to make a fuss, that she would do better to laugh and for her neighbours to think she did not mind, she smiled and shrugged.

He muttered a hushed apology as they walked away, their dance complete, though he did not look entirely sorry. She was at a loss as to what to say or do, was, left wishing for a hole in the floor to appear and swallow her up.

Thankfully, Jane appeared by her side and ushered her into the hall for some air, where they could speak without others hearing.

"You look as if you might faint, Lizzy."

"How dare he?"

Jane only smiled and took out her fan, waving it in Elizabeth's face. "He is in love with you. A man in love ought to be forgiven some impetuousness."

"No! You are wrong!" Elizabeth shook her head. "I know not his reasons. He is all arrogance and conceit. He thinks he may do whatever he..." She wanted to protest more, but her shoulders sagged. "Everyone will be talking of it for weeks."

"Come now! Everyone has had too much wine for it to matter much. There is hardly anyone left here that we know."

"Even so, I am sure they will get to hear of it. Oh, it is so embarrassing!"

"A little perhaps. Though now you will be the girl Mr. Darcy kissed rather than the girl Mr. Wickham threw over for Mary King."

"I shall never live it down."

Jane took Elizabeth's face between her hands, much as Mr. Darcy had just done, and forced her to meet her eyes. "It matters not. Will you listen to me? Where has your cleverness gone? He is in love with you and you with him and, may I say, I mightily approve of your choice."

"I should like to go home," was all Elizabeth could say.

In her absence, it seemed Mr. Darcy had decided that was exactly where they were bound. Her mother and other sisters burst into the hall seconds later, laden with coats and hats, and they were all soon back in the sleigh for the return journey to Longbourn. Mr. Darcy drove them again, his face buried deep in the collar of his coat. He said not a word as he handed all the ladies out.

Elizabeth, torn as she was between anger and confusion, jumped down without assistance and dashed inside. She immediately declared herself ready for bed, going upstairs before Mr. Darcy had even come in.

Yet she did not go to bed. She took a seat by her window and pulled the heavy curtains back so she might see the stars again. Some people believed they could predict the future. But the more Elizabeth looked up at them, the less she knew.

After a while, she heard Mr. Darcy's deep baritone in the hall below. He had such a distinctive voice, and she had come to know it above all others. He was speaking to her father, she thought, and then she heard two sets of heavy steps move towards his library, followed by the peculiar squeak the hinges on that particular door always made when it was opened. Then she heard it being firmly shut.

BLEARY-EYED and with a thick head from too little sleep, Elizabeth came warily down the stairs the next morning, only to be met by the sight of Mr. Darcy's trunks in the hall. He was there too, but not dressed to go yet. She was so surprised she forgot to be angry at him.

"It is Christmas morning," she said. "You are not going?"

"As you see."

"You cannot travel today."

"The turnpike, when I went yesterday, was just about passable. I confess I worry for my sister who is at Matlock without me. My family there are not the warmest of companions. She will not have been as fortunate as I...to have been so graciously received by you all, after the way I previously behaved...well, I have been much humbled. I have said as much to your mother this morning and your father last night."

"You cannot make your servants go so far. Tomorrow should be their day of rest."

He smiled. "You are good to think of them, but know that I am a generous master and they will be well compensated. May I speak to you elsewhere, before I leave?"

She nodded, and they walked down the hall to a small parlour at the front of the house. They passed Jane on their way. Elizabeth had kept Jane awake much of the night discussing everything that had passed. Her sister stifled a yawn and then smiled at Elizabeth in an encouraging way.

Mr. Darcy opened the door for her and shut it behind himself when they were both inside. She put a hand to her chest, feeling it pound in uncertainty, realising only in that moment that he had asked to speak to her alone and that she had followed him, unthinkingly, without stopping to consider what it might mean.

"I was not very gentlemanly last night. You have every right to hate me." He paced over to the window, stopped, and turned. "Do you hate me?"

"No," she said hesitantly. "Though I was angry, embarrassed."

He bowed his head. "I made a dreadful first impression on you, most likely a terrible second, and now an even more awful third. What I would wish for is the opportunity to remedy matters. There was a time when I did not care who I offended, but I have come to admire you. And, through you, I have learnt a different way of seeing the world. It is a gift you have given me—a Christmas present," he said, his voice breaking. "I will be honest and confess I once thought you beneath me, yet now I see your worth. I understand how fortunate I would be…" He stopped to clear his throat. "Mr. Wickham would express himself so much better."

"Perhaps," she said, "but I find I no longer care for his speeches."

"Of that I am glad. I have spoken to your father."

She must have coloured deeply, for he did too.

"Oh, no, you mistake me. I made such a bad beginning that you and I barely know one another. It is too soon, and I would not have you so unsure of me. Though the look of relief you now wear has me perturbed."

Her heart seemed to have moved into her throat, robbing her of speech. She could say nothing but, when he held out his hand, she slid hers into it. It was a glorious feeling when his fingers closed around hers.

"I shall be at Matlock for a time, then Pemberley. After which, I will travel to Town and speak to Mr. Bingley. Be assured, he will call upon your sister at the Gardiners, though after that I intend to leave them to their own devices."

"But that was your forfeit, and it was I who lost the bet. You never told me what my forfeit would be and how I should pay it."

He smiled, the seriousness was gone from his countenance. It had been replaced by a devilish expression. "The forfeit I really wished for, you have already paid."

In his cravat, she found a place to hide her embarrassment and stepped closer to him. "A young lady imagines her first kiss quite differently, Mr. Darcy."

He laughed. "I see my error. May I ask how she imagines her second?"

It was too much for her. She withdrew her hand and stepped back but favoured him with a smile. "A different forfeit, if you please."

"Very well, then," he said, not missing a beat. "What I asked from your father was permission to write to you while we are apart. Your forfeit to me is a letter by return, upon receipt of mine. I will not be happy, madam, if there is much delay in your correspondence. You have seen me at my worst. You know how dreadful my temper will be if I do not have at least a few lines from you by the end of January."

He was as charming in his own peculiar way as a thousand Wickhams, and she suspected she trembled from the force of her emotions. She *was* in love, and what she loved most about him was that he expected no more of her than a letter.

He had come to understand her in these few strange days when he had been trapped at Longbourn. She did not want him to go but wondered if it was selfish to ask him to stay. He left for the sake of his sister. For that, she adored him all the more, but he would be missed.

"We will see one another at Easter," he told her. "You are to go and see your friends at Hunsford. I will go to Rosings Park to visit my aunt there. There is only a lane separating the two properties."

Elizabeth laughed. "As I have been told, many times."

"We might walk together often. The countryside is beautiful. The company I cannot truthfully recommend, but the paths and groves I think you would very much enjoy."

Again, he put out his hand and, again, she took it. The stars knew nothing. Elizabeth could foretell the future from his touch. This was how it would be.

He released her then and, going around the house, quietly offered his goodbyes. When he had finally driven away, Elizabeth escaped back to her room, supposedly to ready herself for church. Instead, she threw herself upon the bed and cried for a good long while, as she had not done since she was a child, till her emotions were spent. She did not rouse until she heard her mother pass by her door, exclaiming to no one but herself.

"Ten thousand a year! Now that makes for a very merry Christmas indeed."

CAITLIN WILLIAMS IS an award-winning author of *Ardently, The Coming of Age of Elizabeth Bennet, When We Are Married,* and *The Events at Branxbourne,* that all spin the plot of *Pride and Prejudice* around but keep the characters just the same. Originally from South London, Caitlin spent thirteen years as a detective in the Metropolitan Police but is currently on a break from Scotland Yard so she can spend more time at home with her two children and write. She now lives in Kent, where she spends a lot of time daydreaming about Mr. Darcy, playing with dinosaurs, and trying not to look at the laundry pile.

AND EVERMORE BE MERRY

JOANA STARNES

Mr. Darcy sends you all the love in the world, that he can spare from me. You are all to come to Pemberley at Christmas. —Jane Austen

*I*s this about right, Mr. Howard, sir? Or should I lower it, do you reckon?" Georgiana heard the third footman ask the butler as she rounded the corner into the entrance hall, arm in arm with her sister. They were just in time to see the young man atop a ladder, seeking to suspend the Christmas bough in the designated spot.

They had amused themselves with putting the finishing touches to it that very morning, she and Elizabeth. Now it stood resplendent with ivy and holly entwined around its hoops, ornamented with red ribbons, gilded nuts, fire-red apples, and the customary sprig of mistletoe.

The latter had begun to be frowned upon in fashionable house-holds, along with the liberties that stemmed from it. Thus, in grand homes, the poor mistletoe was of late grudgingly allowed only in the servants' hall for the so-called *lesser sort* to disport themselves in such an unseemly manner as stealing kisses from young maidens while there were still translucent berries to be plucked. But airs and graces had no place in the Darcys' home—never had and never would—nor would they turn their backs to age-old customs to follow the dictates of fashion. So the old mistletoe was here to stay, both in the Christmas bough and in the servants' hall.

"That will do nicely, Peter. There is no need to lower it," came the instruction, not from the butler, but from the master of the house. Georgiana could not suppress a smile when she heard her sister chuckle.

Still, just as it was proper, Elizabeth waited for their butler and third footman to withdraw before she shared her amusement with her husband.

"For shame, Fitzwilliam," she teased, with an airy gesture towards the kissing bough. "You call this hospitable, having it hung so high? What of our guests who are not quite as tall as you and Richard?"

But Georgiana's brother shrugged and cast his wife an unrepentant grin.

"Then we shall see several gentlemen a-leaping."

"And a partridge in a pear tree," Georgiana added with a giggle, easily swept into their playfulness and the seasonal gaiety.

It was a great joy to return to her childhood home for Christmas to see her dear relations—and to see them so happy. She had missed them grievously ever since she had left Pemberley as a bride and had made her home in Town within easy distance of her husband's place of employ at Horse Guards. Naturally, they met often when Fitzwilliam and Elizabeth were in Town, but they were rarely there ever since the little ones were born.

But now that was of no consequence, Georgiana thought with childish delight. It was in the past. Derbyshire had claimed her yet again now that Henry had come into his inheritance. Their new home was but eleven miles from Pemberley, and she could not be happier.

No, that was false, she thought and smiled. Happy as she was now, her felicity would be complete in five days' time when her husband would be free of the unfinished business that kept him in Town and would come to join her.

"Well, then, what of our walk?" her brother asked, disrupting her ruminations. "I take it that the troop is still above-stairs, readying themselves."

"I imagine so," Elizabeth said with a smile, "or the rest of the house would not be so quiet. I sent them up to dress half an hour ago. With any luck, by now Miss Hughes might have won that battle."

The ever-so-capable Miss Hughes had prevailed, it seemed, upon her charges' penchant for high-spirited procrastination. No sooner had Elizabeth and Georgiana traded their slippers for sturdy boots and donned their pelisses than a cheerful commotion could be heard from the direction of the staircase that led to the family wing.

"Slowly and with care now, if you please. No running down the stairs, and keep a firm hold on the handrail," the governess was heard to say as she admonished her charges towards safety. The wild stampede settled briefly into a steady rhythm, only to revert to an ungoverned rush once the stairs were negotiated.

"Papa, Papa, shall we build a snowman? Can we? Oh, do say we can!"

"No, Georgy, that would take an age. Let us go to the treehouse. Can we climb up, Mama?"

"Papa's shoulders! Best climb on Papa's shoulders," Anne piped up, joining her other sisters in leaping around their father like excitable pups.

Elizabeth made no effort to either curb their exuberance or assist her husband. Instead, she rolled her eyes and smiled as she reached to take her youngest babe from his nurse's arms.

"Do have a cup of tea and a moment's peace, Miss Hughes, at least while there is some peace to be had," she urged, and the elder woman returned the smile and dropped a curtsy.

"Enjoy your walk," she said, opening the door for them and waved at the Miss Darcys as they gleefully tumbled out.

THE FIRST SNOWBALL shot right past her, missing her by inches, and Georgiana drew back from the line of fire, her right hand instinctively covering her mid-section. There was nothing to see, no discernible change, and there would be none for quite some time. She had not told anyone yet, not even her husband. Georgiana smiled to herself.

33

She would tell him at Christmas. Henry would love that present best of all.

Her smile grew wider at the sight before her. There they were, her brother and his happy family, merrily chasing each other through the shrubbery, everyone's dignity abandoned as they dodged snowballs that now flew from all directions. Some came from beyond the azaleas—or rather from beyond the white mounds that stood where the azaleas would be—with no perpetrators in sight, their presence betrayed only by giggles. Some were very accurately sent flying by her eldest niece, who was peeping from behind the artful arrangement of rocks at the furthest end. Fitzwilliam was returning fire with no less skill, and there was Elizabeth, who had once more entrusted her babe to the safety of his nurse's arms and was now dashing from behind a flame-shaped conifer, chased by two ruddy-faced imps who were eagerly taking her back as a target.

The snowball fight had begun as a haphazard whirl of laughter and excitement, but before long an alliance was formed among the scamps, all united in the determination to pelt their parents with as many projectiles as they could fashion. Some snowballs stood the test and flew with uncanny accuracy, while the others disintegrated in the air, for they were little more than scoops of snow thrown without much care for the result but with prodigious merriment.

The parents' alliance was more of the defensive kind. Even now, Fitzwilliam put an arm around Elizabeth and twirled her from the path of a snowball that would have caught her in the face. He offered his broad back to be pelted instead as he sheltered his wife in his embrace before spinning around to chase after their second daughter, scooping up snow for more projectiles as he went.

Georgy ran away with squeals and giggles towards the white-capped hedge, where reinforcements awaited. The other three sprang out with armfuls of snowballs and easily overpowered their compliant father. Moments later, he was on his knees in a melee of flailing limbs and wriggling little bodies, trying to fend off the four-pronged attack by any means possible. Unfair means too, by the looks of it, for Georgiana's youngest niece shrieked with laughter, then lisped in admonishment:

"No, Papa! No tickles. You *promised!*"

"I did no such thing," Darcy retorted, a shocking falsehood from a gentleman who set great store by honesty. His unprecedented slyness received its just reward: the last word of his falsehood turned into a splutter when his diminutive opponents joined forces most effectively and immobilised his arms so that at least three mittened hands out of eight could reach up and scrub his face with fistfuls of snow.

It was rather adorable, Georgiana thought, that for nigh-on ten years her brother had to countenance being increasingly outnumbered. Four girls were born to him and Elizabeth, one after another scarcely two years apart and, after a while, even Elizabeth—cheerful and sensible Elizabeth—had begun to fret that she was too much like her mother and she might never be able to beget a son.

Such worries were eventually shown to be for naught. Little Richard Charles George proved them unfounded and was now squealing in his nurse's arms, turning this way and that. He seemed in equal measure entertained by the goings-on and very cross that he could not take part in the excitement. The fact that he had brought his mother great relief and joy with his arrival nine months ago could not interest him anywhere near as much as his relations' antics, nor could he understand that he was heir to everything the eye could see.

Georgiana's glance softened. Such a fortunate boy, her nephew was! Not just on account of his heritage—she had learned many years ago that, at times, the Darcy heritage could be rather daunting—but for having dearest Fitzwilliam for his father. Her brother would teach his son to ride, hunt, box, and fence, would teach him to love Pemberley as much as he did, and how to care for everyone who made the dear place their home.

Touching as that notion was, the deep emotion stirred in Georgiana's heart was soon conquered by a giggle. Yes, a strong bond would form between them in the years to come, especially if they were to remain outnumbered—which might very well be the case unless Elizabeth took to bringing one son after another into the world.

The rumpus in the snowdrifts seemed to have quietened somewhat once her nieces had achieved their mischievous purpose. Still held to ransom in the shrubbery on his knees, with his face bright-red from the ignominious treatment, Fitzwilliam grinned at his daughters.

"There. Satisfied now?"

The eldest grinned back.

"Eminently, Papa," she declared. "That was *most* satisfactory. For us, at least," she added as she leaned forward to ruffle his hair.

She might have been named after her mild aunt Jane, but she was growing more like her mother every day, Georgiana thought and chuckled.

Fitzwilliam chuckled too as he replied, "Oh, I will have my revenge on the morrow, Miss Sauciness, you may depend upon it. Now be off, all of you. Get yourselves indoors and change out of these wet things. Come now! Lively, lively! Fear me, tremble, and obey," he finished with a playful growl that sent his daughters into another fit of giggles.

Madeleine stifled hers into her hands.

"Papa, you are too droll. Who could ever fear *you?*" she chortled. She reached up to put her arms around his neck and pecked him lightly on the cheek, then set about brushing the snow off his cravat and coat.

Not wishing to be outdone in caring for their dear papa, the other three joined her in the endeavour with as much diligence as they had shown in splattering fistfuls of snow over him in the first place. Then, when the deed was done to their satisfaction, the troop scrambled to their feet, giggling as they sought to shake the snow from their own apparel and long ringlets with great energy but not much effect.

"Chocolate in the nursery, Mama?" Jane asked, with no real expectation of a change in the habitual routine. She was not disappointed.

"Of course," Elizabeth assured her, affectionately patting her husband's back to remove the snow their daughters had missed.

"Will you come up to have chocolate and scones with us? You must! And Aunt Georgy, too," Georgiana's namesake insisted. Once her aunt assured her that she would not miss that treat for the world, the girl scampered away towards the house with her sisters following in cheerful and vociferous pursuit.

Arms linked and still smiling widely, Darcy, Elizabeth, and Georgiana leisurely set off after them, yet Richard decided he had something to say about the arrangement. Utterly out of patience, he released a demanding squeal and stretched his arms towards his father with an insistent clamour of "Da-da-da-da," leaving them all in no misapprehension of his wishes.

With a soft chuckle, his papa complied and came to scoop him up from his nurse's arms. "Not fair, little fellow, is it, missing all the excitement? Never mind, you shall have your turn soon enough, and no mistake. But for now, you might have to be content with a scone in the nursery. What say you? Will that do?"

The tip of a tiny, pink tongue came out between rosebud lips to blow a loud raspberry, and it was hard to tell whether young Master Darcy had found a way to express his views (even if he could not speak as yet) or whether he was just making all the noises expected of a youngster his age. Either way, his father laughed and dropped a kiss on the chubby cheek, then fell into step with his wife and sister as they made their way back to the entrance.

Three footmen were at hand to relieve the cheerful party of their coats, muffs, and gloves and then take the wet garments away to be dried before the fire. Merrily chattering, the three elder girls made their way up the stone staircase followed by Master Richard and his nurse, while the youngest daughter and her aunt were bringing up the rear, holding hands.

As for the remaining two, they seemed somewhat distracted, Georgiana noted with both amusement and affection. The last ones in the entrance hall, Elizabeth and Fitzwilliam were now standing under the kissing bough, eyes locked in a tender gaze and bright smiles glowing in their faces.

Apparently she was not the only one to notice that they were tarrying below. When her brother's hand came up to brush a lock from Elizabeth's brow, then cup her cheek, little Anne asked with considerable concern:

"Has Mama got something in her eye?"

Her parents could not have missed that, surely. Georgiana could have sworn she heard them chuckling lightly just before they kissed. A brief kiss it was, since it had an audience, but although their faces drew apart, they still held each other in a warm embrace as they glanced up as one. By then, Anne had lost all interest and blithely looked away.

"Oh, *that*," she said with a shrug, tossing her hair back. She clasped her aunt's hand and resumed her tottering ascent as she said sagely, "No need to worry, Aunt Georgy, they are well. Do you know, they do that *all* the time!"

A SE'NNIGHT LATER, Pemberley was verily bursting at the seams once all the guests had finally arrived to join them for the Christmas season. Mr. and Mrs. Bingley were there, naturally, and Mrs. Webb (Miss Kitty Bennet as was, before her marriage to the new vicar of Kympton), and Miss Mary (still unwed), and Mr. and Mrs. Bennet. Of all the Bennet daughters, only the youngest was missing from the gathering, for unsurprisingly there was hardly any socialising with Mr. and Mrs. Wickham.

Socialising with Miss Bingley and the Hursts was vaguely more palatable, but not much. Still, they were visiting Mr. and Mrs. Bingley in their new home in the North, so they had to be included in the invitation to Pemberley. The other guest whose arrival brought more tension than pleasure was Lady Catherine de Bourgh, but at least the old family feud seemed to have been put to rest, and it was good to have the opportunity to see more of their quiet cousin Anne.

Their cousin Richard—who could never be described as quiet— was there too, along with his wife and sons, and so were Mr. and Mrs. Gardiner and all their children. Or their offspring, rather, Georgiana amended with a smile. They were no longer children but fully grown, nearly old enough to wed. Yet, not that long ago, *they* were the ones who stood around the table by the window engaged in a lively game of snapdragon.

Now it was her nieces' turn to share in that amusement, and they did so with gusto, cheering and squealing as they competed with their Bingley and Fitzwilliam cousins in reaching out to snatch raisins from the bowl of flaming brandy and pop them into their mouths. In years to come, their brother would undoubtedly join them in the daring pursuit, but for now he was asleep in the nursery, far away from the noisy disport.

The children's faces glowed with the flicker of the flames and the thrill of the valiant endeavour, and of all the people gathered in the room, it was only Mrs. Bennet who was too busy fretting to appreciate the spectacle.

"Oh, this game!" she cried, her kerchief aflutter, and likewise her spirits. "It sends shivers down my spine every time I see them at it. Why must they expose themselves to danger?"

"Nonsense, madam," Lady Catherine declared. "Danger, indeed! Does them no harm to learn to avoid mishaps. It will harden them a little. They are brought up too soft."

"But their hair could catch fire!" Mrs. Bennet protested. "Or their sleeves. Or they could burn their mouths! Oh, no, no. I cannot watch. It tears my nerves to shreds! Mr. Bennet, pray tell me when they are done with this savagery so that I can look again." Yet she could not look away, nor could she help exclaiming, "Oh! That was close. Too close. Mark my words, Lizzy, this will end in tears!"

Yet it did not. It ended in more giggles and a clamour for another game once all the raisins had vanished into eager mouths.

"Bullet-pudding! Can we have a game of bullet-pudding now, Mama?"

"Oh, yes, Aunt Lizzy, bullet-pudding! The best game," young Charles Bingley cried in support of Madeleine's suggestion. "We never play it elsewhere. 'Tis the best part of coming to Pemberley!"

"I am very glad to hear it," Elizabeth said and stood. "If this is the best part, then we cannot disappoint you."

She affectionately ruffled her eldest nephew's ever-so-curly hair, then went to tug the cord and make arrangements. In due course, Mrs. Reynolds appeared with a large pewter dish piled high with flour, and a young maid followed on her heels bearing a tray with round-ended butter knives. With eager exclamations of delight, the children rushed to choose one and gathered round the table, ready to cut the "pudding".

"There you go," Darcy said, grinning widely as he placed the bullet on top, and then he gave the signal for the children to begin.

Elizabeth stood by to lend assistance, cajole some, and urge others to wait for their turn to cut the "pudding." Georgiana watched them do so in diverted expectation of the moment when one of them would inevitably make the bullet drop and would then have to seek it in the flour—not with their tiny hands, though, but their mouths.

Her eyes crinkled at the corners and a smile fluttered on her lips at the recollection of her brother's deep discomfort when this boisterous and untidy disport was brought to Pemberley on the first Christmas after his marriage to Elizabeth. If snapdragon was a Darcy tradition, the game of bullet-pudding was a Bennet one. There was no doubt that her brother had struggled to take it in his stride and keep his mien impassive while the Gardiner children had sought the bullet and sent clouds of flour floating in the pristine drawing room at Pemberley.

These days it was only Lady Catherine, Miss Bingley, and Mrs. Hurst who scowled, shuddered, and sniffed in disapproval. Fitzwilliam would not bat an eyelid. Rather than wincing from a distance, he sat at the heart of the cheerful disturbance, holding Anne on his knee to give her a sporting chance against her older and much taller sisters and cousins. He laughed when she cut the "pudding" too close to the bullet and made it roll down into the flattened side of the pile of flour. He was still laughing when she turned towards him, giggling, her face a while mask from the eyes down but the bullet proudly exhibited between her teeth.

"Mind you do not swallow it," he said, holding out his palm for the bullet, and rolled his eyes while reaching into his breast pocket for a kerchief to wipe the flour off her chin and chubby cheeks.

Georgiana's smile widened. How grand it was to see him delighting in a pastime that had once made him cringe—how grand indeed to see her beloved brother following his wife's example and learning to enjoy life to the fullest!

Georgiana's affectionate glance drifted from her brother to her dear sister, and a warm glow of gratitude filled her heart. It was all thanks to Elizabeth. It was thanks to her that this room, once so painfully quiet, was now abuzz with good cheer and excitement. It was thanks to her that Pemberley was a true home again—that love and laughter abounded in Fitzwilliam's life.

Not that they had not had their stormy moments. Sparks had flown at Pemberley often enough. In fact, truth be told, their worst disagreement had been on her own account—or rather, on account of her matrimonial intentions.

Her gaze settled lovingly upon her husband, who stood by the fireplace in an animated conversation with Mr. Gardiner. Even now after all these years, Henry did not know the half of it. Once matters had settled onto their happy course, she had chosen to keep silent on the subject of Fitzwilliam's first reaction to Henry's courtship, for there really was no reason to foster any coldness between her brother and the man she loved.

Nevertheless, the truth was that Fitzwilliam had begun by uncompromisingly opposing Henry's suit, so much so that a severe disagreement had flared between her brother and Elizabeth once Henry had made his intentions known. He was sent away with a civil request for some time so that the matter could be given due consideration, but later that day, Fitzwilliam had not minced his words in his conversation with his wife.

This conversation Georgiana had inadvertently overheard. That is to say, she had inadvertently overheard its beginning from the morning parlour separated only by a door from Elizabeth's sitting room. But then, much as she knew she was at fault to eavesdrop, it was her very future that was under discussion, so she did not walk away. Not even when Elizabeth's voice had risen, to sound bitter and harsh and unlike any tone she had ever used in speaking to Fitzwilliam before.

"Of course," she had almost sneered. "You married beneath you, but heaven forfend that your sister should make the same mistake. Or worse still, your daughters, I imagine."

"That is uncalled for," Fitzwilliam had retorted just as hotly. "Unfair too, and well you know it. Besides, there is naught amiss with Vernon's connections. 'Tis his commission I object to. In case you have not noticed, we are still at war. Should I countenance having my sister broken-hearted should her betrothed lose his life in the Peninsula?"

"Better break her heart by forbidding the betrothal altogether, then?"

"Yes!" Fitzwilliam had fiercely shot back. "While he is still in active service, yes, to my way of thinking. And I shall not disguise my views under vague assurances and all manner of falsehoods."

"Indeed, why should you?" Elizabeth had scathingly replied. "We both know that disguise of every sort is your abhorrence."

At that, Fitzwilliam's tones had cut like steel.

"So much for forgiveness and a happy union. Must I do penance for a foolish speech for as long as I live? What of a pound of flesh instead, would that satisfy you better? Or would you rather bring this up whenever suits and hold it against me forever? Have it your way, then, Elizabeth. Nurse old grievances till they fester, if it pleases you. I thought we had moved past this long ago. More fool me, it seems. Excuse me."

Nothing was heard afterwards but heavy footfalls and the slamming of the door.

Eventually, when Georgiana could bring herself to join her sister, she found Elizabeth morose and silent. Yet as the day wore on and the shadows lengthened, her ill-humour gave way to anxious glances darting to the door…then to restless pacing and complaints that the snow had melted so there would be no visible trail to follow and no way of ascertaining where the vexing man had gone.

Before long, a footman was dispatched to inquire at the stables. He returned to say that the master must have gone on foot, for all the mounts were accounted for.

Even later still, when the outdoor and house servants who had formed a search party began to file in, still with no tidings of Fitzwilliam's whereabouts, to her further dismay, Georgiana discovered that Elizabeth had also vanished.

It was another hour before her sister had returned with muddy skirts and no pelisse, just a shawl wrapped around her shoulders, to let them know that—praise be!—he was found, and to ask two sturdy footmen to escort her to the folly on the other side of the lake, where Mr. Darcy waited with what she feared was a broken ankle.

"He had clambered up the rocky outcrop behind the folly and slipped. Not from the top, thank goodness, so he is not severely injured. Still, the physician should be summoned."

It was only later, much later, when the house was at peace, that Georgiana could reflect with a brimming heart over the events of the day. It spoke volumes of their attachment—the fact that, even after their bitter disagreement, her brother should have bent his steps towards the folly he had commissioned for his wife, and that she should have been the only one who knew where to look, and the one who found him.

At long last, Fitzwilliam was brought home and made comfortable in the sitting room he had so tempestuously quitted, and Old Mr. Allen came to prod his ankle and declare it was not broken, just very badly sprained. Nevertheless, that foot should not bear any weight for at least a se'nnight, so Mr. Darcy should employ a pair of crutches or countenance making use of his late father's Bath chair.

"A se'nnight in a Bath chair," Fitzwilliam observed when the physician was gone, having left draughts for the pain and instructions on how they should be taken. "I expect you will say 'tis just what I deserve," he ruefully added with a sheepish glance towards Elizabeth, who was busying herself with placing another cushion under his elevated foot and then wrapping a quilt around him.

Yet, as he spoke, she lost all interest in her employment. She released the edges of the quilt and, careless of Georgiana's presence, she reached to cup his face in her palms and leaned down to kiss him almost savagely.

"Do not dare give me this sort of fright again!" she said in a fierce whisper and kissed him once more, whereupon Georgiana saw merit in swiftly retreating, a warm smile on her lips and the sting of tears in her eyes.

Yet it was a long way to the door, and she could not fail to hear the earnest words that followed: "This is what matters, Fitzwilliam. *This,*" Elizabeth whispered between kisses. "Love—however long we are allowed to keep it. There are no certainties in life. But all of us should be permitted to grasp love with both hands if we are fortunate enough to find it."

Needless to say, Elizabeth's words of wisdom had once again borne fruit. His concern and reservations notwithstanding, Fitzwilliam had given his consent. A month later, Georgiana was betrothed to her beloved Henry.

And yes, her brother was in the right as well—she had not drawn an easy breath until the end of the gruesome conflict on the Continent. Yet, if she had to choose all over again, she would not have chosen differently.

With a start, Georgiana brought herself back to the present. The game of bullet-pudding had come to an end and, with their parents' assistance, the children were busily dusting off the flour. Henry's conversation with Mr. Gardiner had come to an end as well. He came to sit beside her and took her hand.

"Are you growing tired?" he asked with great solicitude.

Georgiana shook her head and smiled. A month ago—nay, a mere fortnight—she would have said he could not possibly love her more, nor could he be more mindful of her comfort. She could see her error, now that Henry knew she was with child.

Her husband returned her smile as he settled back into the cushions, at her side.

"I imagine I would do well to start taking instruction from your brother. Or at least watch and learn. It will stand me in good stead one day."

"True," she said, squeezing his hand.

She glanced at Fitzwilliam just as he relinquished a wriggling Anne from his hold. He set her down and came to sit beside Elizabeth on a nearby sofa, only to find their second daughter scampering towards them.

"Can I take my cousins to the music room, Mama?" she eagerly asked. "Would anyone mind if I played a carol for them?"

"Not at all, my love," Elizabeth assured her, and Georgiana could not fail to wonder yet again at her namesake's delightful confidence and willingness to play and sing in such a large gathering.

Not in the least daunted by the prospect, her second niece turned to her cousins.

"Come! Mama says we can," she chirped and led the way through the large, wide-open doors into the adjoining music room.

She dragged the seat closer to the instrument and cast a winning smile towards the footman who had obligingly fetched her a cushion. With the man's assistance, she perched herself upon it while her young relations gathered round, some standing beside her, others huddled together on a sofa or sitting cross-legged on the floor.

The older members of the audience sat up to listen too. They were soon rewarded with rather faltering but not discordant notes and a clear voice that did not falter:

> *Lo, now is come, our joyfulest feast!*
> *Let every man be jolly,*
> *Each room with ivy leaves is drest,*
> *And every post with holly,*
> *Though some churls at our mirth repine,*
> *Round your foreheads garlands twine;*
> *Drown sorrow in a cup of wine,*
> *And let us all be merry.*
>
> *Now all our neighbours' chimneys smoke,*
> *And Christmas blocks are burning;*
> *Their ovens they with baked meats choke,*
> *And all their spits are turning.*
> *Without the door let sorrow lie,*
> *And if, for cold, it hap to die,*
> *We'll bury it in a Christmas pie,*
> *And evermore be merry.*

The appreciative claps could not quite drown out Lady Catherine's disapproving sniff.

"Hm! I find it highly inappropriate that a child of eight—that a young *lady*, regardless of her age—should sing about drowning one's sorrows in a cup of wine or burying them in a Christmas pie," she declared, glaring at her nephew and her niece by marriage.

As wise as ever, Elizabeth feigned selective deafness and kept her eyes averted from their imperious relation as she whispered to her husband so quietly that Georgiana could scarce hear her.

"Oh dear. I hope Georgy will not take it to heart. I should have advised her to keep to *God Rest Ye Merry, Gentlemen* or some such traditional carols."

"Nothing can daunt her," Fitzwilliam replied, his voice just as low but unmistakably filled with affectionate pride. "She takes after you, thank goodness."

Still keen to have her say, Lady Catherine scowled.

"I wonder who has taught her this unbefitting song," she enunciated, but Elizabeth knew better than to rise to the challenge, least of all on Christmas Day.

"Not me," she informed her husband in another whisper. "For once, I am utterly blameless. It was Mrs. Reynolds," she resumed, in response to his diverted glance. "I heard them singing it in the pantry together the other day when they were making ginger biscuits."

"I always knew the dear lady was worth her weight in gold," he replied, reaching up to brush some specks of flour forgotten on Elizabeth's cheek.

From her own seat, Lady Catherine spluttered.

"Really! Is *that* the example he is setting? Disgraceful conduct in a man his age, and moreover in company!"

But to Georgiana's way of thinking, her brother was setting an excellent example to the assembled company, children and grown men alike, when—commendably undaunted indeed—Georgy moved on to play another tune. He cast a warm glance towards his second daughter, then stroked Elizabeth's hand with his thumb and cheerfully exclaimed:

"Ah, the *Barley Mow*. Whoever can resist it? May I have the pleasure, Elizabeth?"

With her smiling concurrence, they rose and, still holding hands, they sauntered towards the music room, only to find the youngsters haphazardly pairing and joining them in the dance with little skill but great enthusiasm. Promptly, Mr. and Mrs. Bingley joined them too, and Richard and his wife soon followed. Georgiana arched her brows towards her husband, teasing challenge in her eyes.

"If you should wonder, no, I do not think this is too sprightly, and I would dearly love to dance—if only anyone should ask me."

He had no need to be told twice, and they left the drawing room together—yet Georgiana did not miss Lady Catherine's second splutter:

"I *beg* your pardon? Why, the very notion, Mr. Bennet! I most certainly shall not!" she exclaimed with energy as she tossed her head back, making her long feathers flutter. From that, Georgiana concluded that Mr. Bennet had kindly asked her to stand up with him for the sake of family harmony and was unceremoniously refused.

Not in the least put out, the older gentleman shrugged.

"Well, that is that. What say you, my dear, shall we?" he asked his wife instead, and before long the drawing room was left to Lady Catherine, Miss Bingley, and the Hursts; even Anne had chosen to walk into the music room and eventually came to partner her own namesake and join her relations in their gambols.

Georgiana cast an almost pitying glance over her shoulder towards the three ladies who had chosen to remain in the drawing room in stony silence, lips pursed and countenances set in frosty dignity. Yet a fraction of a second later, their collective air of poise and good breeding was completely lost. Georgiana very nearly chuckled to see them jump and scowl when Mr. Hurst suddenly awoke from his habitual after-dinner slumber.

"Aye, and a damn fine evening too, what, what?" he exclaimed—ill-advisedly, given the sacred day and the company of so many children —then sat up and drained his glass of port.

"Oh, Mr. Hurst..." said his wife, her dramatic sigh barely audible over the cheerful tune that still filled the music room mingled with a great deal of good-humoured chatter.

JOANA STARNES LIVES in the south of England with her family.

Over the years, she has swapped several hats—physician, lecturer, clinical data analyst—but feels most comfortable in a bonnet. She has been living in Georgian England for decades in her imagination and plans to continue in that vein till she lays hands on a time machine. She is the author of eight Austen-inspired novels: *From This Day Forward—The Darcys of Pemberley*, *The Subsequent Proposal*, *The Second Chance*, *The Falmouth Connection*, *The Unthinkable Triangle*, *Miss Darcy's Companion*, *Mr Bennet's Dutiful Daughter*, and *The Darcy Legacy*, and one of the contributing authors to *The Darcy Monologues*, *Dangerous to Know: Jane Austen's Rakes and Gentleman Rogues*, and *Rational Creatures*.

THE WISHING BALL

AMY D'ORAZIO

Know your own happiness. You want nothing but patience—or give it a more fascinating name: call it hope. —Jane Austen

DECEMBER 2014

*I*f it had been up to him, the whole ordeal of decorating for Christmas would have been delegated to the designers who had recently redone his office complex.

His younger sister Georgiana wouldn't stand for it, though. She insisted on a fire in the fireplace, cookies in the oven—okay, not actually cookies but a cookie-scented candle—and Mariah Carey wailing about all she wanted for Christmas.

And now there was a present in his hand. Fitzwilliam Darcy looked down into the Georgiana's eager face and felt that sinking feeling that he had already missed his mark. Was he supposed to have gotten a present? Now? Almost an entire month before Christmas?

"Well!" he said with as much forced joviality as he could muster. "What is this, Georgie?"

Georgiana beamed with delight. "It's a wishing ornament! You use it to wish for the upcoming year," she explained with all the earnestness of a teenage girl who still believed in happy endings. "Cara put one on her tree last year and she got a boyfriend, like, two days later. And she hasn't had any acne since!"

He gave the box a cursory glance, noting the words "genuine silver plate" emblazoned on the side. "Well, who could doubt the mystical powers of something purchased at Things Remembered?"

Georgiana's face fell, and she snatched it away from him. "I know it's stupid."

"No, it's not. I'm sorry, I'm in a terrible mood." He took it back from her. "This is really sweet, honestly. Thank you. I love it."

"It's just...don't you ever wish we had more?"

He felt it, that familiar guilt and worry welling up within him. When their parents died, he was left as her guardian and had invited her to live with him to keep her from having to go off with some distant relative. He knew he did well in terms of seeing to her education and making sure she was fed and protected and watched over... but it was her happiness that he had no idea how to ensure.

"Sweetheart, we have it great. Look around us. We live in an amazing city, in a beautiful home without any of the cares and worries—"

"We have money," said Georgiana flatly. "It's not the same. I just wish things were more...busy and bustling sometimes."

He knew exactly what she meant. There was a reason that depression rates soared around the holidays. It was that endless niggling that everyone else was out having a wonderful time with family and loved ones while you gamely tried to make things look special. "It's hard to bustle with just the two of us."

"I know. Anyway, it's late. I'm tired."

"No, wait a minute," he protested. "Let's do the ornament thing. What do we do with it?"

She shook her head. "No, it's no big deal." She leaned in and gave him a kiss on the cheek. "This was fun."

He didn't stop her, feeling as though he had messed up enough this night. He stood there until he heard the shower turn on a few minutes later. He left the great room then, making a brief stop in the kitchen for some hot chocolate laced with a liberal dollop of peppermint rum and then retiring into his study.

The ornament remained with him, still enclosed in its box. He decided to open it. It took some doing—the box had been closed with one of those clear cellophane stickers that were invented to secure Fort Knox—but eventually he was able to tear the box open around it and extract the ornament.

It was heavier than he had expected it to be, a silver orb comprised of two hinged halves that opened to allow the wish to be inserted. It had been monogrammed already with his own initials, making him shake his head. Georgie had made such an effort, and he'd treated her so dismissively.

The shower was off now, so he went up to her room, knocking gently on the door.

"Come in." She was seated at her vanity when he entered, her hair wrapped in a towel.

"Hey, I just wanted to say sorry for being a grumpy jerk about this ornament. I saw how you got it monogrammed—it's great. The perfect addition to our decorations. Want to go put it on the tree together? Maybe put our wishes inside of it?"

"Monogrammed?" She gave him a look. "I didn't have it monogrammed. What, like a *D* or something? They probably all came with an initial on them and I just happened to grab the *D*."

He looked down at the ornament again, puzzled. "No, not just a *D*. *FGD*, my full monogram is engraved on this thing...in a manly font, no less."

"Let me see." She rose from the vanity and came to take the ornament from him, examining it closely. "Whoa. That's so weird."

"Come on. You know you did it."

"I didn't!" She looked at him, eyes wide. "Ask Cara. She was with me when I bought it."

"You really didn't?"

"I promise," she said. They both stared at it for a minute until Georgiana added, "I guess it's a mystery."

Darcy looked down at it again, recalling his difficulties in opening the box. *It had been sealed rather tightly, hadn't it? But what else could explain the fact that his monogram was on it?*

"Are there any wishes inside of it?" she asked. Her tone turned teasing. "That would be really weird. Like maybe someone wrote, 'Dear Wishing Ball. This is Will Darcy, and I haven't had a date in five years. Please, please, have mercy on me!" She giggled.

He was glad to see that her melancholy had dissipated, and he didn't mind her teasing a bit. He played along, giving her a little shove with his elbow. "I've been busy, okay?"

Darcy pressed on a little clasp to pry it open, revealing a blue velvet interior. It was surprising —and yet not—to find a scrap of paper enclosed, folded into the smallest square possible.

"Oh my gosh! There *is* a wish in there already! What does it say?" Georgiana was practically salivating with the delicious peculiarity of it all.

Darcy unfolded it slowly. Truth was, it was starting to weird him out. "Probably some general sort of message, like a fortune cookie. They probably all come with something in there about fortune in the new year or something."

"Do they all come engraved with *FGD* too?"

He didn't deign to reply to that. Surprisingly, what was written had been written by hand.

"Wow, that even looks like your writing!" Georgiana exclaimed. "Now I am freaking out!"

"It just looks like a man's writing," he said. "Any man's penmanship. Not necessarily mine."

"No," she insisted. "Look at the *I*. That's how you do *I*'s, and I've never seen anyone else write that way."

He scowled. "Dad taught me that way. I guess...the schools in England teach it like that, but here...they do it differently here."

"So some other man...another man, with the initials *FDG* and a tendency to make the letter *I* like he went to prep school in England, bought this ball, wrote a wish, placed it inside, then sealed it up, and returned it. Then I, your sister, just happened to come along and buy it? That's your hypothesis?"

Georgiana stood, her hand on her hip, shaking her head. "Uh-huh, Will. Doesn't hold water. Face it—it's fate. Fate is coming after you."

"You're being silly," he told her, trying to ignore the small voice inside him that agreed with her. There were too many coincidences here. But no—there had to be a logical explanation. Richard playing a joke maybe? Was Bingley somehow involved?

He supposed that actually reading the message might shed some light on the subject. If it said something on the order of, "Beware the woman in orange!" he'd know it was Richard, teasing him that Caroline Bingley's pursuit of him was heating up again.

He unfolded it and read it, scratching his head after he did so.

"Read it out loud," Georgiana said. "I can't see it."

"It says"—he cleared his throat—"'I wish it would happen for me.'"

"What?" Georgiana looked at him for a moment and then shook her head. "You wish what would happen for you?"

"I don't know. Remember, I didn't write this. So how do I know what it means?"

She ignored him. "Only you would make such a non-specific wish. You wish *what* would happen? Didn't you just say you thought everything was great?"

"I didn't write this," he reminded her firmly.

"But the monogram is—"

"Somehow Richard is behind this," he told her. "He's probably been on pins and needles for days waiting for this to come to fruition. You know how he is."

"Oh." She had a crestfallen look. "I'm sure you're right."

"I'm sure I'm right too," he said. He leaned over, kissing her head. "You need to get some sleep."

Ten minutes later, he was back in his study queuing up a movie while he tapped out a message on his phone.

FD: *Nice with the ornament. Had us going for a bit, I'll admit it.*

His movie had just come on when Richard replied.

RF: *IDK what you mean*

FD: *the wishing thing*

RF: *???*

FD: *the ornament you had engraved with my initials*

RF: Right. To match the hankies I'm embroidering for you. WTF?

Darcy paused a moment. Was Richard being serious? Normally, once one of his jokes was brought to light, he'd call his victims chortling with glee and amusement. This time he seemed genuinely baffled.

FD: It really wasn't you?

RF: Nope. Sounds like it got you good though. Wish I thought of it what-ever it was

Another pause, and then Richard texted again.

RF: Gotta bolt. Lissette is here. TTYL

FD: later

Setting his phone on the table, Darcy sank a bit into the couch cushions, feeling exasperated and uneasy. He could already tell it would be a long night. He was exhausted but not sleepy, a combination he detested but which was becoming all too familiar.

He had no idea what was causing his frequent insomnia lately, but night after night saw him sitting on this very same couch watching pointless movies and wishing the nights weren't quite so long. He had developed quite a sympathy for older people like his aunt Catherine, who sounded almost boastful when she whinged about her inability to have a full night's rest. She scoffed at the notion of eight hours sleep but, in a way, he could understand it now. It seemed the ultimate divine irony that when a person arrived at the stage of their life in which they had ample time to sleep, their brain chemistry or whatever would prohibit it.

The worst was that during the night his other feelings, his restless sort of ennui, came at him in full force. He really had no idea what was even wrong; he just had a constant sense of waiting. For what, he had no idea, but he felt like his real life was out there, waiting to be lived, and he was only marking time until he caught up with it.

In that sense, he understood completely the meaning behind the words on the little paper. "I wish it would happen for me." Maybe it was something to do with being almost thirty, but he was exhausted with the uncertainty of his life. He had too many questions and not enough answers. Would he ever fall in love? Would he always be alone? Would he marry someone awful who would take his money and drag him through a bitter divorce? Would he ever have children? Would he have children that turned into drug addicts and screamed "I hate you" at him? What if he finally found a wife he adored and then she died?

Too many questions. No wonder he couldn't sleep. It seemed so easy for other people: meet, date, fall in love, marry…give birth to adorable cherubs who played soccer and drew pictures of dinosaurs with thick rectangles for legs…who refused to eat vegetables and went trick or treating and learned to ride bikes and roller skate…who took tests and went to proms and made varsity teams and graduated and went to college and soon had babies of their own. Normal life.

He had picked up his laptop as he mused, absently flicking through web sites: ESPN, CNN…and Facebook.

He never looked at Facebook, having been coerced to join it by Bingley at the beginning of the year. Bingley had been enthusiastic about it, going full bore into liking and following and updating his profile picture and his status with an almost manic glee. Darcy had, on several occasions, debated unfriending him—if he saw one more picture of Bingley's hand holding a cup of coffee and musing about the wonder of Starbucks in the morning, he couldn't say what he'd do to him. But unfriending him seemed too hostile, so he simply stopped looking.

Tonight though, he was bored and lonely and it seemed worth a look so he started scrolling. Moments later, he nearly dropped his laptop, sitting up and exclaiming aloud, "Who did that?"

His own profile shot had been changed to a picture of a baby. A baby dressed as a snowman, dark curls pressed into a top hat (which it was reaching up to try to remove) with an orange nose painted onto its little face and greasepaint "buttons" on its bare belly. A jaunty red scarf completed the effect.

"Richard," Darcy muttered, wondering how long it had been like this and how many people had seen it. A quick glance at his feed showed that the photo had received seventy-three likes … Did he even have seventy-three people who could see his stuff?

There were comments too. Jane Bingley (Who?) said "Totally stealing this idea!" and TomFanny Bennet (Who?) said "When are you coming to see us?" Georgiana Darcy said "I have the sweetest nephew ever!" —*What?*

Why would Georgiana say this kid was her nephew? What was going on here?

His heart began to pound even as his head insisted that this was all some ridiculous sort of joke. He began to move through the pictures, seeking clues for what in the world was happening.

The next picture showed two kids, the baby and another little guy —a toddler—hovering over the newborn with a clear sense of disdain. "He looks like me," Darcy mused aloud. "Sort of." Actually there was no "sort of" about it. The kid was a dead-ringer for him as a child.

He continued scrolling, moving back in time on his Facebook page. The baby was replaced by a woman, standing sideways with a massively swollen belly jutting out in front of her. Lots of likes on that one, along with Bingley's comment: "Stop taking pictures and get her to the hospital!"

Then the toddler kissing her belly...and a picture of Darcy himself, taken from what must have been the woman's vantage, looking down at him. He was grinning like a completely besotted goofball, his lips puckered toward the belly.

"I've never grinned like that in my life," he told the screen.

Finally there was a full-on shot of the woman, much less pregnant this time, although still with a little bump. She was cute, he supposed, although not really his type. Too short, and that wild, curly sort of bohemian hair wasn't really his thing. Although...it was pretty. It looked soft, albeit frizzy. She was holding his hand and the toddler was in his other arm. They made a nice-looking family. Whoever did this was pretty good with photoshop.

He kept scrolling, still working backwards. The belly disappeared altogether and the toddler reverted to babyhood. He liked trains apparently; his room was decorated in Thomas the Train. And there was a picture of Darcy sitting hunched over a train table, playing with him. *Christmas again? Looks like it.*

Who is this kid? Where did these pictures come from?

I've been hacked. He heard about these Facebook hacks all the time, and obviously that was what happened here.

"Change my password," he muttered going to his security settings and clicking around before realizing he had no idea what his current password was and therefore attempting to change it would only get him locked out.

And he didn't want to get locked out. He wanted to keep looking. He knew he should be completely weirded out but he was intrigued. Intrigued...and also a bit jealous. He liked this life he was looking at. He wished it was real. He'd play trains with this kid, gladly.

For a brief moment, he wondered where his old trains were. He'd been quite a collector when he was young and had saved it all thinking that one day his son would—*Stop it!* He scolded himself. *Not real. You don't have a son and no one wants to play trains with you!*

One of the comments suggested to him that the boy was named Jaz. *Seriously? Who named this kid Jaz?* Unless...well, his grandfather's name had been Jasper, and it had been his father's middle name. Was this kid named Jasper for his own grandfather?

Time kept rolling backward. He saw more pictures of himself along with the woman and Jaz...they took some sort of vacation, him in the sand with both of them... *Okay, when she isn't pregnant, this woman has one seriously hot body.* "And this is after she already had Jaz," he said aloud, then wondered if he was crazy for talking about these people like he knew them.

It was the next picture that truly arrested him though. It was just him and the woman. He didn't know who had taken it. They were sitting at a table, very close together. She was smiling at the camera but he was smiling at her, his arm around her. It didn't take too much to see that he was completely in love with her, and he could see why.

Her hair was beautiful, cascading down over her shoulders and his arm, but her eyes...her eyes were the most gorgeous he had ever seen. Rich and dark and large and lined with thick lashes. His heart beat fast just looking at them.

What really made them extraordinary though was the expression. Was it always so easy to know a person just from their eyes? This woman's eyes told everything about her. That she was warm and loving and kind. That she had a great sense of humor and didn't play games with people. For her eyes alone, he desperately wanted this woman, whoever she was. He felt a rush of yearning, of desire for this unknown woman.

He suddenly realized he could find out exactly who she was. He moved his cursor around, looking for the tag. Finding it, a name came up: Elizabeth Darcy.

"Elizabeth Darcy?" He half-scoffed. He clicked her name, hoping to find her page and shed some light on this whole puzzling absurd…thing.

Error. The page you are looking for cannot be found.

He frowned, went back to the link, and tried again. Same result. Couple more clicks yielded exactly the same thing.

He opened another tab and googled Elizabeth Darcy. There were several, it seemed, but none that made any sense to his current dilemma. There was a Beth Darcy on Facebook, but she looked about twelve and didn't resemble his Elizabeth in any way.

He decided to keep looking at the pictures.

Some family gathering was the next picture, but who were all these people? Richard with Lissette…was she pregnant too? Bingley with a good-looking blonde on his arm, a *definitely* pregnant blonde. Georgiana was there, sitting next to some trampy-looking girl about her age. Lots of young women; they filled the room. Lots of smiles all around, though, including on Georgiana's face. Too bad it wasn't real; Georgiana had always wanted to go to some big family holiday get together as opposed to just the two of them sitting in some five-star restaurant.

The next picture seemed to be the same gathering. An attractive woman who looked around fifty and wearing an extremely low-cut sweater was holding Jaz, who had red lipstick marks on his head. A man sat beside them, sort of scholarly-looking older man, smiling down at Jaz. *Grandparents?*

He kept going, watching as Jaz got smaller, took his first steps, and celebrated a birthday with Elizabeth laughing beside him. Wow…it was a moment frozen in time and yet he could almost hear it, the silver bell of her laughter. He wanted to laugh too, just looking at her joyous face.

In the next shot, he saw why she was laughing like that. Jaz had eschewed the typical first-birthday tradition of wiping cake all over his own face, choosing instead to smear it on Darcy. In another shot, the boy appeared to be licking Darcy's cheek. Evidently he'd realized that frosting was good stuff. Darcy chuckled looking at him, almost feeling Jaz's small baby hands holding his head still while he attacked his dad's face.

In subsequent shots, Jaz got his first tooth and sat up for the first time. Then Elizabeth was pregnant again, wearing leggings and Darcy's Cambridge sweatshirt for what looked like a room-painting project. A grainy picture before that, black with some fuzzy ghost-like images and a caption: "IT'S a BOY!!!" Darcy felt weirdly choked up to see that.

Then came the pictures of just him and Elizabeth. Picnics in the park, hiking among autumn leaves, some river in England…evidently she was a nature girl. They had honeymooned somewhere with a big coral reef, evidently done a good bit of snorkeling.

He had never really thought about it before, but it would be nice to have a wife who enjoyed doing fun things like he and Elizabeth appeared to do on Facebook. "They're friends, too," he told the screen. "Best friends from the look of it."

Wedding day. Some weird impulse made him skip over those pictures. "Can't see the bride before the wedding," he murmured. "I wouldn't want to know what her gown looks like."

A picture of Elizabeth's hand, his mother's ring proudly displayed with: "SHE SAID YES!" That got one hundred and twelve likes along with a few comments like "Man down!" from Richard and "I'm so happy, I'm crying!" from Jane Bingley. Jane Bingley always commented on their stuff, so she and Elizabeth must be good friends, he thought.

He couldn't take his eyes off that hand wearing his mother's ring. He found himself reaching out and laying his fingertips on the screen.

Of course the ring was in his safe, and he had no doubt that it was still there... *This is just a dream...right?* Obviously he had fallen asleep on the couch and was dreaming all of this.

He then remembered something Bingley once told him. Everything a person did on Facebook was recorded—the time, the date...

He debated a second before quickly clicking on his account summary and activity log.

A quick glance showed him, yep, Fitzwilliam Darcy joined Facebook on January 4, 2014. He skipped over the stuff in between to see that his last activity had been at 8:49 p.m. on December 12, 2018, when he had changed his profile picture.

He inhaled sharply.

What sort of...this was weird! It had gotten too weird and he needed to just forget about it all. It was a dream. Nothing but a crazy, sharply detailed dream.

Temptation attacked him... He wanted to find out more about the woman who would become Elizabeth Darcy. Had he met her before and just didn't remember her? Or maybe he'd meet her... Where would he meet her? When would they go out? What about Jaz?

A strange, painful pang hit him: Jaz didn't really exist. Snowman Baby didn't exist either. Jane Bingley, the happy family stuff—none of it was real. He swallowed against the pain of loss that thought produced. What if Elizabeth didn't exist, either?

NOT REAL. He woke the next morning on the couch in his study. His laptop was on the floor, having apparently slid from his lap at some point. Didn't seem to have any harm done to it; it woke from sleep mode much more easily than Darcy himself did.

The temptation to log onto Facebook immediately was overwhelming, but he resisted for a good hour or so, reminding himself every other minute that he had dreamt the entire thing. A weird dream brought on by some sort of holiday melancholy and the peppermint rum he'd put in his cocoa.

As he sat down to lunch, however, he couldn't help himself. The intention to check email somehow became a log on to Facebook. The page loaded slowly while his heart pounded in his chest.

His corporate mugshot stared grimly back at him. Total number of friends was seven, total pictures posted was one, the mugshot. No status updates.

His disappointment lasted for most of the day until it occurred to him that night, in the midst of another bout of insomnia, that she might be out there. Every day that passed would bring him closer to the reality of knowing her.

He began to imagine scenarios for meeting her. While Christmas shopping somewhere in the city, he scanned the crowds hopefully, once following a curly haired woman twelve blocks before she glanced over her shoulder and he realized she was a teenager. Feeling like a creep, he turned on his heel and walked away fast. He ducked into busy coffee shops, scanned the theatre diligently when he and Georgiana saw the *Nutcracker* and studied the ice skaters at Rockefeller Center more than he ever had in his life. He watched the *Today* show religiously, looking at the people in the background while Al Roker did his schtick.

He even went so far as going to Times Square for New Year's Eve. It was horrid, with drunken people everywhere, pressed up against him as he moved through the crowd with Bingley. Bingley loved it, of course, commented several times on the "energy" of it all, but he had a purpose.

Alas, it was a purpose that went ungratified.

By Valentine's Day, he had essentially given up. Bingley had ended his holiday fling, so he was despondent too. They ordered in some Thai food and drank too much while toasting the single life and watching action movies on TV.

MARCH 2015, ORLANDO

Bingley waited until they were deplaning to hit him with the news.

Darcy shot him down immediately. "You want to buy a place here? Bingley, that's a terrible idea."

"The market is oversaturated," Bingley said, rolling his luggage past a stand of coconut candies, stuffed alligators and oranges. "Great properties are a dime a dozen, and I thought it would be fun to—"

"You can't look at it like that." Darcy groaned. "Yes, they have a surplus, but you would have to see a ten percent growth over the next five years to recapture…"

Darcy continued on, delivering a veritable dissertation to Bingley on how and why investment property in Florida was a bad, bad idea for him. Bingley blithely whistled as they walked along, ignoring Darcy completely.

"I want a place where my friends and I can go, do some fishing, and have a good time," Bingley explained when Darcy had said his piece. "You can't do that with bonds and securities."

"Fine, go fishing. But rent! You don't need to buy a house to go fishing."

"No, but I do need a place to lure the ladies." Bingley gave him a wag of his eyebrows. "Can't get laid from an investment spreadsheet, can I?"

Darcy shrugged, feeling peevish. "You'd have to ask the guys who date your sister."

"Harsh!" Bingley laughed.

They were nearly out of the airport then, the muggy heat assailing them as they left the artificial cold of the airport. They had rented a car and trudged toward the place where they would find it.

It was Darcy's habit by now to scan the crowd, both at the baggage claim and as they left the airport. A foolish habit because Elizabeth Darcy didn't exist and probably never would. It gave him a sinking sensation every time he acknowledged it to himself, but it was getting better. He was learning to accept his lonely reality.

It was these thoughts that were in his mind when Bingley informed him of his plans for the evening. "House of Blues, good band… We'll have fun, meet some girls."

Darcy groaned, thinking that it sounded like the complete opposite of anything he'd be interested in doing. But he reminded himself he would never have a wife if he never forced himself to meet women. So he'd go.

House of Blues was the antithesis of anything Darcy had ever, in his life, found even remotely pleasurable. It was tacky and overly commercialized; the music was too loud, and the room was too crowded and too lit by neon, and he hated it all with a passion.

"These girls are Georgiana's age," he exclaimed looking around him.

"Spring break for some places," Bingley grinned. "Just make sure to check ID before you take anyone home with you." He then burst into maniacal laughter, knowing that no one was less likely to end up with someone than Darcy.

"Let's just go have a drink somewhere else. Somewhere with actual adults in it."

"Are you kidding? Look at the women in this place—uncommonly hot, Darcy. Don't be so determined to hate everything. You might surprise yourself and actually have a good time once in a while."

Darcy tried one last time as he ordered their drinks at the bar. "Didn't you want to get an early start tomorrow? Out on the bay by seven, wasn't that the way?"

"Yep." Bingley was already eagerly eying the talent on the dance floor. "Good thing we're young, right? Guess your insomnia really comes in handy in situations like this."

An hour later, Darcy had a headache that throbbed in time with the pulse of the loud, techno music. A drunken bachelorette party had descended upon the area where he sat, commandeering the rest of the chairs from his little table and subjecting him to way too much of their conversation, which mostly centered on sex, male genitalia, and the butts of the men in their respective lines of sight.

"Darcy!" Bingley arrived with gusto, sloshing his drink into his friend's hair before attempting to sit where there wasn't any seat. "Oops! Hold up." He turned, somehow located a chair and pulled it up.

"Are you wasted?" Darcy frowned at him.

"I'm drunk with love." Bingley sighed.

"Not again." Darcy shook his head. "Bingley, I forbid you to bring someone home."

Bingley sat up straight. "I don't even want to bring her back to the condo. This is my future wife, Darcy, and I can't sully that with a cheap bar hook-up."

"Future wife?" Darcy moaned. "Okay. Well, now that you've met a future wife, can we leave?"

"No way! I just came over to get you out there with us. She's right over there… This is her friend's bachelorette weekend."

Bingley gestured, and Darcy obligingly looked where he pointed. Hot blonde at nine o'clock—she was vaguely familiar somehow. Did he know her? He puzzled over it a moment before dismissing the idea. In any case, she was certainly a beauty. Totally Bingley's type.

Bingley sighed, clearly rapturous. "Florida is just full of beautiful women, isn't it? All so tan…"

Darcy gave a quick glance around him, seeing orange-hued skin and bright, too-tight clothing, much of which resembled workout apparel—and that did not include the bachelorette party.

"I assure you, you've managed to find the only beautiful woman among this tribe of phallus-festooned hussies. Can we please just go?"

"A few more dances, okay? I know you're bored—you should dance with her sister! We can all hang out together!"

"What? Absolutely not."

"Yes!" Bingley was warming to the idea. "Wouldn't it be better to just dance than sit here nursing a watery drink in the corner? Come on. Her sister is cute and seems like a lot of fun."

"You think I'm going to dance in a place like this? Forget it. I'm not sure which of these…charming ladies"—making it clear he thought they were anything but that—"is her sister, but I will go ahead and give you a comprehensive 'hell no' that covers the lot of them. Sound good?"

"Works for me." A feminine voice came from behind him.

He whirled around, and his heart plummeted into his shoes. For a moment he could do nothing but gape at her stupidly.

It was Elizabeth.

His eyes moved over her, rapidly seeing the hair, the body, the eyes…all of it, just like he knew it would be. Her. His Elizabeth, Elizabeth Darcy, right here, standing in front of him. All of his searching, the waiting…she was right here, in Florida of all places.

Disbelief and excitement dumbfounded him; he could not even speak.

Excitement gave way to alarm as he realized she had pushed by him, leaving him. Without thinking he reached out, grabbing her by her arm. "Wait! Elizabeth!"

She whirled around, jerking her arm out of his grasp. "Hey!" She poked her finger into his chest. "Back off!"

"Sorry!" He reached for her again, but she took a step away, nimbly evading him. "Elizabeth, please, just stay a minute."

She glared at him fiercely. "I don't know who you think you are, but you'd do best to get out of my way immediately, if not sooner."

This was said between clenched teeth, and he added "perfect smile" to the list of things he found beautiful about her. He had never felt so stupid in his life, staring at her, beauty and fury personified. Her eyes were magnificent, ablaze with anger, and her full lips were parted, releasing huffs of indignation.

He thought it was entirely likely he should be feeling terror. Instead he was overwhelmed with desire as well as concerned that he would forget himself and crush her to his chest in a passionate kiss, thus getting himself punched in the process.

His emotions prohibited rationality so, completely incongruously, he found himself sticking his right hand out toward her. "I'm Will Darcy."

She crossed her arms across her chest. "How do you know my name? Have we met?"

"I… Yes, we've met. In a manner of speaking." He shook his head, still feeling a bit stunned. "I just can't believe you live in Florida."

"If you've met me before, then you should know I don't live in Florida," she snapped at him.

"You don't? Where do you live?"

She stared at him.

"Listen, I'm sorry about the…about the grabbing thing. I was just really excited to see you." He smiled then. "I'm harmless, really."

She was still giving him an incredulous look and appeared to be slowly widening the gap between them.

"How about this," he suggested, edging a bit closer to her. "I'll put my hands behind my back. That way, if I do anything else to upset you, you've got a free shot. Sound good?"

"Free shot?" She raised one eyebrow. "Where?"

"Anywhere you want," he told her, putting his hands behind him as promised. "Stomach, groin, face... Try to spare the face though, please. I have a really irritating cousin who will want explanations if I return to New York with a broken nose."

She stared in surprise for a moment before laughing. "So we're both New Yorkers then."

"You live in New York!" His hands flew forward, reaching for her, but he stopped himself just in time. He carefully folded his arms behind himself again. "That's great!"

She frowned at him, but the fury had disappeared from her eyes.

Just then, Bingley, who had sidled off sometime during the altercation with Elizabeth, returned with his new love at his side. She was blonde and angelic and gave them a kind smile, oblivious to the psychotic undercurrent around her.

"You must be Darcy," she said warmly, extending her hand. "I'm Jane Bennet, Elizabeth's sister."

His eyes went wide. *Jane Bingley!* He nearly laughed. Well, Bingley might think he met his future wife often enough but, in this case, it seemed he would be right.

"It's great to meet you, Jane," he said warmly.

Bingley beamed at Jane before leaning in to hug Elizabeth. "Well, this is great! Elizabeth, I'm Charles. Great to meet you!"

A few moments of chat ensued. Elizabeth continued to look warily at Darcy, and Darcy continued to scramble mentally for a way to prolong their encounter. He had to get to know her more than a two-minute conversation in a bar afforded.

It was Bingley who had the solution. "How about a late dinner, ladies?"

"No, I don't think we can..." Elizabeth's protests were halted as soon as she glanced at Jane, whose eyes were clearly pleading her to go. "Maybe just something quick."

They found themselves in some sort of horrid chain diner-like place that boasted an all-you-can-eat breakfast bar which was open and available twenty-four hours a day. Darcy himself would have preferred to lick sand than eat from it, but Bingley exclaimed in delight and tucked in. The rest of them drank coffee and got to know one another.

Darcy was content to sit and stare at Elizabeth, lost in his admiration of her until she said, "Would you mind?"

"Would I mind what?"

"Perhaps you could blink or something once in a while." She gave him a raised eyebrow look. "Are you recently released from prison or something? It's like you've never seen a woman before."

He chuckled. "No, I haven't been to prison."

"It's weird to sit here totally silent. We should have some conversation, not just you *staring* at me while I pretend not to notice you."

"So let's talk," he said. He cast about for a suitable topic. "Do you often come to Florida?"

"First time," she said. "My friend Charlotte is getting married, and apparently Disney is her idea of an amazing bachelorette party."

Conversation began in fits and starts, but soon they were talking as if they had known one another for some time.

Elizabeth, he learned, worked in publishing. "At the most junior level," she said. "Terrible pay, long hours, and very little respect, but I get paid to read all day."

The more he learned about her, the more he knew *this was it*, and it was real. The particulars didn't really matter.

What struck him was the feeling of connection to her, a similarity in mind and understanding that he knew would serve them well as they deepened their relationship.

Then a terrible thought struck him: what if she did not fall in love with him? Maybe she was already involved with someone. Maybe she was already in love.

The conversation had faltered, one of those natural pauses in conversation. He took a sip of his coffee and said, "Can I ask you something?"

"Sure."

"When we're back in New York, will you go out with me?"

She looked a little awkward.

"Are you with someone? I mean, you know, dating or maybe serious or even—"

"No, no. It's not that," she said. "I'm... I'm single."

"You're not interested," he said, trying not to show his keen dismay. "I improve on further acquaintance. Really I do, I promise. Look how much more you like me already; you hated me in the club, and now we're sitting here having a nice conversation. Just imagine how much better I'll get once I'm back home."

She laughed. "I'm sure you will. No, it's just I've had some bad experiences with men lately and my New Year's resolution to myself was to just take a break from the whole scene."

"Sounds reasonable," he said. "How about a permanent break?"

"A permanent break?"

"There are two ways to have the break you promised yourself," he told her. "One is no men at all, and two is just one man: the right man. No heartbreak, no complications, just falling in love, and building a life together."

She laughed. "That sounds great—in theory. However, experience has shown me that every guy is the right guy at the beginning."

"I'm the right guy for you," he told her, his voice quiet but determined. "Beginning, middle, and end. You might not realize that yet, but it's true. Give me a chance and I'll give you a happy life."

"This is insane." She laughed uncomfortably. "You don't know me, and I don't know you. What on earth would make you say these things?"

"Just trust me. I know."

She blushed, staring at him. Her mouth opened and she formed several words, beginnings of sentences, but never uttered a sound. Finally she said, "Do you always come on this strong?"

"No, never."

"Really?"

Without taking his eyes off of her, he said, "Bingley."

Bingley managed to tear his attention away from Jane. "What?"

"Would you describe me as the sort of man who comes on strong to women?"

"What?" Bingley laughed. "Is this a joke of some sort?"

"No," Darcy said, his eyes still on Elizabeth. "Do I? Do I tend to come on strong to women?"

"Have you ever even asked a woman out?" Bingley said, shaking his head. "No, Darcy doesn't come on strong. In fact, he doesn't really come on at all. The women generally do the work for him while he tries to escape them."

They all laughed a bit, and then Jane and Bingley turned back to their own conversation, leaving Darcy and Elizabeth to theirs.

"A chance," he said. "A date, maybe two. The rest will take care of itself."

She considered it a moment while he held his breath, at last saying, "Okay. When we get back to New York, we'll go out."

DECEMBER 2015

And now, here we are, he thought, smiling as he unwrapped the wishing ornament. Right where we were meant to be.

Not that it had been completely easy. The chemistry between them was undeniable from the start, as well the friendship they formed easily and naturally. However, they had had more than a few explosive arguments. She misjudged him, and he tended to say whatever he thought with little-to-no forethought. They worked it out, though, and every time, they ended up closer than when they'd begun.

He had known he would fall in love but, somewhere along the way, he'd realized he was already there. Not too long after that, she returned his feelings and it had been bliss ever since.

So tonight, one year to the day when he had opened his own ornament...

He looked at the smooth heavy orb in his hands, feeling a thrill of anticipation mingle with nerves and anxiety, and just about everything else.

It was a new wishing ball that he held in his hand; his was already on the tree. The one in his hand was engraved with her initial—just an E—and contained a little surprise inside of it.

"So can I come in there now?" She smiled as she came into the room.

"I'm ready for you." He handed her the ornament. "This is for you."

69

"It's cute," she said. "Little silver bauble, huh? Should I just hang it on your tree?"

"It's a wishing ornament," he explained. "You put your wish inside and it comes true."

She shook it. "Sounds like something is already in there. You didn't steal my wish, did you?"

"I'm hoping what's in there is a wish for us both."

"For us both?" Her teasing tone left her as realization dawned on her, and she looked more earnestly at the ornament. "Oh."

"Why don't you open it and look?"

She gave him a smile that already looked a little tremulous before pressing the little latch and revealing the contents. It was a slip of paper and he noted, with some satisfaction, the fleeting expression of disappointment on her face.

She unfolded the paper and laughed a little before reading aloud the words he had written: "You didn't really think I'd put a ring in a Christmas ornament, did you?"

"Fitzwilliam Darcy you are a—" The words died on her lips as she raised her eyes and found him on one knee in front of her. Tears immediately formed in her eyes, making them look shiny and even more beautiful than usual. "Oh, Will…"

He took her hand, kissing it gently before looking into her eyes. "Elizabeth, I love you. And I know beyond any doubt that you are the one for me. I don't want anything else but to make you happy for the rest of your life." He kissed her hand again before whispering, "Please marry me."

It wasn't until several hours later that he was able to get a picture, a close-up of her beautiful left hand wearing his mother's ring.

DECEMBER 2016

"Look! Our ornaments!" Elizabeth pulled both of the ornaments out of the storage box, smiling fondly.

"Hard to believe that, last year this time, we were just getting engaged."

"The year has flown by."

"Best year of my life."

"Mine too, honey," he said, before kissing her lightly on the nose. He reached up to put his ornament on the tree.

"Wait." She put her hand on his to stop him. "Don't you want to look inside?"

"You just got it out of the storage box. How could it have something inside of it?"

She shrugged. "Just check."

He looked at her carefully, seeing nothing but benign good humor in her eyes. He knew what he'd wish for, though it was something of a secret wish. Although they had only been married since June, he wasn't getting any younger and he was ready to start a family.

He and Elizabeth hadn't really talked about it yet; they were still practically on their honeymoon, and Elizabeth hadn't really given any indication that she was ready to move on to parenthood.

But... there were a few nights where ideas of birth control had been tossed to the wind. The pill made Elizabeth sick, so she'd stopped taking it but planned, in a somewhat vague way, to try something else. They were going to use condoms in the meantime, but there was that one night in the living room when he hadn't felt like going upstairs to get one, and she had just laughed and suggested that they roll the dice.

He was sure nothing could have come of it though. It was only once or twice...three times, tops.

With growing excitement, he pried the ornament open, all the while wondering if there was any brand of those pregnancy sticks which would somehow fit into a three-inch sphere. There wasn't; instead, the ball contained a piece of paper, folded up. He undid it, staring at it in bafflement.

It was black with a small white blob in the middle of it. Elizabeth leaned over his shoulder, staring at it with him. "Is that...?" He asked in confusion. "What is this?"

"It's an ultrasound," she told him, happy tears shining in her eyes. "That's a baby, our baby. We're going to be parents!"

"We are? It is?" He held up the picture to stare at it more closely. "Is it...it's a boy, right?"

"They can't tell yet. It's very early on. I had no idea. I thought I was just coming down with a cold or something."

Chills raced over his skin as he looked at the little white blob. *Jaz. I know it's you, Jaz. How are you doing, buddy?*

A strange tightness came into his throat as he looked at the little blob, imagining the years of trains and soccer balls and birthday parties, kissing boo-boos...teaching him to drive, warning him not to smoke, showing him how to tie his tie... He could hardly wait to get started.

"Are you happy?"

"Am I happy?" He pulled her close to him. "I'm ecstatic."

DECEMBER 2025

"Daddy...Daddy...Daddy...Daddy! Watch me! Daddy! Daddy, are you looking? Daddy! Daddy, look at my cartwheel!"

He turned, watching as four-year-old Ivy carefully put two hands onto the floor, kicked one leg up dramatically, and then stood, flinging her hands into the sky with all the flair of an Olympian. "Taa-daa!"

"Very good, sweetie," Darcy replied automatically.

He couldn't find the wishing balls, which was strange because they always put them in exactly the same box for storage. He began to dig, once again, through the tinsel.

"No, it wasn't good," said six-year-old Jack, a.k.a. the Snowman. "It was stupid. Cartwheels are supposed to have both legs in the air like a wheel."

"You're stupid," said Ivy as she launched into a series of pirouettes. "I can do cartwheels how I want, and how I want is with one leg."

"Kids," said Darcy absently, "don't call each other stupid."

"But Dad, she doesn't even do it right," Jack said, clearly aggrieved.

A bit of a dust-up ensued, ending with Darcy giving all the kids ice cream and calling Lizzy on her cell phone to find out when she would be coming home.

She was at a bit of a reunion: her friend Charlotte—the one whose bachelorette party had been going on in Florida that fateful night so long ago—was finally on the happier side of a long, bitter divorce battle. From the sounds on the phone, it seemed the ladies were re-creating their more bawdy memories from that night.

An hour later, the kids settled into a sugar haze in front of the television, Darcy resumed his search, but the wishing ornaments were not to be found. When Elizabeth arrived home an hour later, he had nearly torn the attic apart and still hadn't found them.

He went to her, kissing her and noticing how tired she looked. "Too much party, love?"

She gave him a look. "I don't really know, to be honest. I spent most of my time in various discreet locations nursing Lilly. She must be going through a growth spurt. This is the quietest she's been all night."

He looked down at his fourth child, his second daughter. Two daughters, two sons. The joy that they and their mother brought him was unfathomable, immeasurable. There was nothing he'd found in life that could compare to the sweet feeling of having their small hands enclosed within his or feeling their limp bodies deep in sleep against his chest. That thought in mind, he picked Lilly up, snuggling her to his chest while smiling apologetically at Elizabeth's protests.

"So, I've looked everywhere and I can't find our wishing ornaments," he told her. "They're nowhere to be found."

"They're in with the crystal snowflakes. I distinctly remember putting them in there."

"Nope."

He detailed for her all the various placed he'd looked. She looked concerned but soon changed her clothing and joined him in another search. Lilly obligingly remained asleep while her parents undertook their fruitless task.

"I don't know what to say," Elizabeth finally admitted. "They should be right here. I remember putting them here myself when we took the tree down last year."

"But they're gone."

Both of them stared, baffled, at the storage box until Elizabeth shrugged. "Oh well. I think Red Envelope still has them. We'll get new ones."

"I—" He stopped himself.

Elizabeth never knew about that weird night over a decade ago when he'd seen their sons and her and the life he knew was out there for him. He had never wanted to influence things or push things in a direction that they weren't meant to go but, so far, it had been exactly as he'd seen it.

He and Elizabeth had dated, fallen in love in the usual way—well, maybe not completely usual, but close enough.

It had been Elizabeth's idea to name their firstborn Jasper. "Old fashioned names are hip," she told him. "And it's in your family." It had been Elizabeth's youngest sister Lydia who first called him Jaz. Lydia had a very irritating habit of shortening everyone's name (Elizabeth was Liz, Jane was Juicy-J, Bingley was Bing...eleven years later and she still called him Fitz or F-schizzle despite his many reminders to stop). In Jaz's case, however, it was cute and fitting, and so it stuck.

Having been born in November, Jack had an early and intense love of snowmen. He had *Frosty the Snowman* read to him obsessively, he had a stuffed snowman he took with him wherever he went, and his first word was even "snowman". It was Elizabeth's friend Charlotte who came up with the idea for the snowman picture; she painted his little belly and face and took the photograph to promote her burgeoning photography business.

But now his ornament was gone. What could it mean?

Elizabeth laid her hand on his arm. "No big deal. We'll get new ones."

"New ones?"

He considered it. After all, he'd never really purchased the first one, had he? He liked to believe that it found him somehow. Getting another one seemed pointless.

In any case, what more could he wish for? He looked around him. A beautiful home, a loving wife he adored beyond reason, and four wonderful children. There were things to hope for, certainly, but wishes?

"No, I don't need another one." He smiled down at his Elizabeth. "You don't need a wishing ornament when all of your wishes have already come true."

AMY D'ORAZIO is a former scientist and current stay-at-home mom who is addicted to Austen and Starbucks in equal measure. While she adores Mr. Darcy, she is married to Mr. Bingley, and their Pemberley is in Pittsburgh, Pennsylvania. She has two daughters devoted to sports with long practices and began writing stories as a way to pass the time spent at their various gyms and studios. She firmly believes that all stories should have long looks, stolen kisses, and happily-ever-afters. Like her favorite heroine, she dearly loves a laugh and considers herself an excellent walker. She is the author of *The Best Part of Love* and *A Short Period of Exquisite Felicity*.

BY A LADY

LONA MANNING

And sometimes I have kept my feelings to myself, because I could find no better language to describe them in. —Jane Austen

"*Y*ou grumble, old fellow, merely because you have heard other husbands do so, and you assume you must do likewise. You think it belongs to your station in life."

Fitzwilliam Darcy raised his eyebrow at his cousin, either in exception to being called "old" or to signify his disagreement that he had nothing to remark upon in the behaviour of his wife.

"I merely said that some patience was required when Elizabeth visits her favourite bookstore. We ought to have been on our way by now."

"The servants and your children set off two hours ago and will be at Hunsford well before sunset," replied Colonel Fitzwilliam. "As for you and I and Elizabeth, why be in a hurry for our reunion with Aunt Catherine?"

"I enjoy a looking around a bookstore as much as the next person, as you know, but once we have begun a journey, I like to complete it."

"Seriously, Darcy, if this is all you have to complain of in married life, you have nothing to complain of at all. I have stayed with you at Pemberley often enough to bear witness that your wife does not nag you, she never keeps you waiting when dressing for dinner, and she remains as lovely to this day as when you wed. And to crown it all, she is shopping for second-hand books, which pleases *my* sense of thrift, at least."

Just then, Elizabeth reappeared from the throng in Lackington's bookstore, looking well pleased and holding a few volumes in her hands. At the sight of her dark eyes sparkling with pleasure and her smiling face, Darcy abandoned any pretense at impatience. After four years of marriage, she still had the power to enchant him.

"Nearly ready, gentlemen! Just look at my finds! A first edition of *Evelina,* with the most elegant binding! It has such beautiful endpapers! And this!" She held out a neatly-bound volume. "The history of Lady Jane Grey! And look at the author's name—Theophilus Marcliffe!" She laughed and repeated the name with emphasis: "Theophilus Mar-cliffe! I picture an earnest old Scots divine with a nose like a parrot's beak sitting in his untidy study with books piled high all about him."

"But a minister would be certain to append *Doctor of Divinity* after his name," said Darcy. "I fancy Theophilus Marcliffe is a pen name. The author may be an impoverished university student or even a lady."

"Oh, I shall be so disappointed if there is not really a person named Theophilus Marcliffe!" replied Elizabeth, although her eyes twinkled as she smiled up at her husband. "I shall make my purchases and let us be gone, then."

"Only these two?"

"Heavens, no!" Elizabeth turned, and Darcy beheld an older man standing behind her, holding a tottering pile of books so tall that he had to peer around them to see where he stepped.

"So many?" asked Darcy as they all made their way to the sales counter in the middle of the main floor. "Where do you propose to keep all these books, my dear? Are you going to have them sent to Pemberley?"

"And send some coals to Newcastle, while you are at it," put in the Colonel. "You have a splendid library already at Pemberley."

"No, dear, they are coming with us to Rosings. I need all these books if we are to spend a fortnight there," Elizabeth replied. "Rosings has an extensive library, but I suspect Lady Catherine has not added a single volume since your uncle passed away. I know from my first visit that no novels pollute the shelves, so I must bring my own supply! Was your cousin Anne forbidden to read novels as a girl?"

"I am afraid that I cannot answer your question," said Darcy.

The older man reached forward and deposited the pile of books on the counter just before they threatened to topple over.

"Sir, thank you again for coming to my aid." Elizabeth smiled. "You are so very kind."

"My pleasure, madam," came the response. "And if I may observe, madam, it is generally known in the publishing trade that 'Theophilus Marcliffe' is the pen name of a well-known philosopher whose writings do not earn enough to keep his family."

"Books on philosophy are a thing I always *mean* to read but never buy," said Elizabeth. "No wonder he must take up his pen to write popular histories."

"If it is any consolation, ma'am, the philosopher in question does have a most prodigious nose."

"I am satisfied," declared Elizabeth. "I shall forgive him on account of his need...and his nose."

Darcy seconded his wife's thanks and cordial introductions were exchanged. Elizabeth's benefactor was discovered to be James Montgomery, a publisher of children's books.

"Children's books!" exclaimed Elizabeth to Mr. Montgomery. "I quite forgot—I wanted to get a picture book for our son William. Something to help him learn his letters."

"As it happens, ma'am," interposed the older man genially, "Lackington's has some of my books. Would you allow me to make a gift—one moment, if you please—if you would do me the honour..." and he dashed off to an upstairs gallery while Darcy and Colonel Fitzwilliam exchanged wary smiles. Elizabeth did have that effect on discriminating gentlemen.

The picture book was obtained, the bill was paid, and Darcy was finally able to bundle his wife into the carriage for the trip to Rosings.

Darcy noticed that Elizabeth was quiet and thoughtful during the ride, and he was not surprised when she raised the topic of Anne de Bourgh again once Colonel Fitzwilliam had composed himself for a nap.

"My dear, I will confide in you that I intend—it is my hope, at any rate—to become better acquainted with your cousin Anne. You said that you did not know if she reads novels. What *do* you know of her? After all this time, all I know is that she does not play, or paint, or draw—so what does she do? I have resolved that getting to know her better shall be my special undertaking this Christmas."

"This is very good of you, Elizabeth. My poor cousin leads a sadly constrained life. When she was a child, she was not allowed to run about the lawn, or ride, or swim. She was not permitted to own a kitten or a puppy. But what has inspired you to undertake this benevolent mission?"

"Because I harbour an uneasy conscience as regards her."

"Why in the world should that be, Elizabeth?"

"I shall confess it to you: on first acquaintance, I saw she was sickly and cross-looking, and I held her in something very like contempt."

"Whilst I observed you at Rosings, my dear Elizabeth—and you *know* how I was watching you most carefully," he said, taking her hand in his, "you showed the utmost courtesy to my cousin. And your fearlessness with my aunt went a long way to causing me to fall in love with you."

"My conscience does not reproach me on the score of what I *did*," Elizabeth whispered, "but of what I *thought*. I was uncharitable. I was unkind. I looked down upon her. You were not there when I first dined at Rosings, for example. Anne sat beside me and, because she said not a word to me, I said nothing to her. I derived more pleasure from disliking her and building on my prejudice than in trying to draw her out. I could easily have made the attempt. Instead I told myself she was stupid, dull, and haughty."

"I would describe Anne as shy rather than haughty. Of course, she is Lady Catherine's daughter, so one can hardly wonder that people assume Anne is proud rather than merely reserved," said Darcy.

"It is possible to be both! Both proud and reserved, that is," Elizabeth laughed softly, giving her husband a meaningful smile followed by a peck on the cheek. "My point is, my *own* character held me back from understanding *hers*. When I was one-and-twenty, I believed that someone who says little must have little to say. I know better now. What if your poor cousin *does* have thoughts, and hopes, and wishes? And, as we know, her *mother* wished that you and she...."

"My dear, have I not assured you that Anne felt nothing for me in that way? I am certain of it." Darcy's voice dropped to a husky whisper: "We were only cousins to each other, nothing more."

"In the first place, she might guard the secrets of her heart, and *you* would be none the wiser," his wife murmured back. "I thought I saw her smile once when Mr. Collins dropped a hint about 'a much-anticipated and well-matched union.' But a smile could mean anything. She might find Mr. Collins's manner of speaking to her mother as ridiculous as I do.

"Even granting the assertion that a woman could know you and *not* fall in love with you—which I have ever found to be a ridiculous supposition—surely Anne *must* want for something more in life than to go for airings in her phaeton with her old governess and sit every evening with her mother. She would be a total imbecile if she did not want something more."

Darcy squeezed her hand sympathetically. "Your anonymous philosopher might say that many people would gladly change places with her to be the heiress of Rosings."

"The heiress of Rosings she may be, but she is more like the prisoner of Rosings...while I am the happiest creature in the world," Elizabeth murmured, cupping her hand against his cheek. Life has blessed me immeasurably, my darling. I have you, and little William, and the baby, and a beautiful life. Therefore, I have resolved, since Lady Catherine has been gracious enough to extend the olive branch and invite us all for Christmas, the least *I* can do is make an effort to befriend her daughter."

"I see, and what better way for Mr. Bennet's favourite daughter to show friendship than through books and reading?" Darcy murmured, pulling at the lap robe which lay over his wife's skirts and tucking it more firmly around her against the winter chill. "Now I understand why you insisted on buying so many books."

Elizabeth sighed and laid her head on his shoulder. "Perhaps they can form some basis for conversation between us for, if they do not, I do not know how I shall penetrate her reserve."

"What about my aunt? Do you intend to make her fall in love with you as well? Or do you still resent her for the things she said prior to our marriage?"

"Truly, I harbour no resentment—or hardly any," Elizabeth declared stoutly. "Your aunt had her reasons to be dismayed at the thought of our alliance, however ungraciously she expressed them. I ruined her dearest plans and hopes. However, she was *almost* civil to me when she came to visit us last year."

"And she grew rather fond of our William."

"Who would not?" declared Elizabeth with the happy complacency of a proud mother. "She gave me prodigious amounts of advice on how to care for him and bring him up, which I have been careful to ignore altogether. For this visit, I have a baby daughter for my calling card. Surely Lady Catherine will dote on her. Everyone does, after all. Your aunt must unbend at last once she meets her namesake."

With that happy thought, she snuggled against her husband and enjoyed a little nap until they reached Rosings.

ELIZABETH BENNET DARCY seldom found herself at a loss for words or in want of fresh subjects of conversation, but within a quarter of an hour of being in Anne de Bourgh's company, she already despaired for the success of her holiday scheme. Anne had so very little to say! She returned all of Elizabeth's enquiries with only a "yes" or "no," and any questions Anne *might* have posed in return were all forestalled by Mrs. Jenkinson, who hovered by the heiress's side.

"I trust you had a pleasant journey, Mrs. Darcy?" "Is the weather more severe in Derbyshire?" "How long did you stop in Hertford-shire?" "I trust you left your family in good health?" "I believe you have relations living in London?"

Anne merely nodded and smiled when Mrs. Jenkinson compli-mented Elizabeth on her children. "Little Catherine bids fair to be a beauty! And William is the very image of his father!"

Miss de Bourgh looked even more frail than Elizabeth had recalled. Darcy's cousin was well below the middle height and exceedingly slender. She was pale and sickly; her features, though not plain, were insignificant. Her brown hair was elaborately curled and dressed, suggesting that she spent a good part of her morning suffering the ministrations of a lady's maid. Her light grey eyes seldom met Elizabeth's sparkling dark ones.

Feeling that she had nothing to lose, Elizabeth unwrapped the little parcel she had brought to the drawing room and offered the first volume of *Evelina* with a cordial smile and a "My dear cousin, this story was ever an old friend of mine" and "We have our own copy at Pemberley, yet when I saw these beautifully bound volumes at Lackington's, I could not resist purchasing them for fear they should fall into unworthy hands. Will you do me the honour of giving it a home?"

Any reaction from Miss de Bourgh would have gratified Elizabeth —even a refusal or a coldness might have given her some notion of where she stood with the daughter of her hostess. She was relieved when Anne looked at first surprised, then wary, and then slowly extended her little hand to accept the volume. The "My gracious, how thoughtful" and "What a pretty little book it is, too" came all from Mrs. Jenkinson, while Anne caressed the handsome leather cover of the book. Then Anne slowly opened it, to look at the title page.

"This volume does not bear Madame D'Arblay's name," said Anne. "This must be the first printing of the work, I perceive, when it was anonymously published."

Now it was Elizabeth's turn to be silent, but from surprise.

"Thank you, Cousin Elizabeth," said Anne. "This is...this is very special, and I shall always keep it with me in my bedchamber."

"What are you speaking of, Mrs. Darcy?" came the voice of Lady Catherine de Bourgh from across the room. "I must know what you and Anne are speaking of."

Anne sighed faintly and hid the book in her shawl.

Elizabeth rose and crossed the floor to join her hostess. "We were talking of books, Your Ladyship. Your library here at Rosings is very handsome. I believe I derive as much pleasure from the sight of books and having them around me as I do from reading them. What is a home without books?"

"I recommend to all young ladies that they set aside some portion of the day for reading," Her Ladyship returned. "Had Anne's health permitted, she would have improved her mind through extensive reading, but she suffers from weakness of the eyes."

"Oh, that is most—"

"Having weak eyes, in itself, is not undesirable in a young lady," continued Her Ladyship, "but the greatest care must be taken not to squint, which creates furrows in the brow."

"Indeed, madam," said Elizabeth. "Prolonged thought of any kind is a hazard to an unwrinkled complexion."

"Sir Lewis de Bourgh ensured that our library was well stocked with improving works suitable for young persons. I do not like to see girls reading anything of a satirical or radical nature, of course. I abhor satire."

"Yes, madam," Elizabeth said meekly, recollecting herself. She reminded herself she truly intended to keep the peace at Christmas. "I should be most gratified if your ladyship would be so kind as to recommend any particular authors or titles from your own library."

"Ah! Well!" Lady Catherine coughed. The truth was, she was not a great reader herself, usually content to look over the periodicals in an off-hand way. "Perhaps we shall have the gentlemen read aloud to us in the evenings—that is, when you are not playing for us, Mrs. Darcy. I trust you have not neglected your instrument?"

"Fortunately, on account of having Georgiana with us at Pemberley, I have a strict taskmistress. Georgiana and I encourage each other, and I have learned some new pieces with which I hope to entertain Your Ladyship whilst I am here."

"It was wise of Darcy to leave Georgiana to spend Christmas in London with Mr. and Mrs. Bingley. She cannot expect to find a suitable husband if she resides solely in the country. My own daughter's indifferent health, of course..."

"Yes, Your Ladyship." *Pray do not reflect aloud on Darcy's folly in choosing me, instead of your daughter.*

Fortunately, Mrs. Jenkinson interjected with "Where do the Bingleys live, ma'am?" which prompted Lady Catherine to give her opinion on the desirability of various London neighbourhoods and streets, followed by enquiries into Mrs. Jane Bingley's housekeeping and the management of her servants.

Elizabeth answered a long succession of impertinent questions and disagreed with nothing while her mind wandered ahead to dinnertime, when her friend Charlotte Collins and her husband would arrive.

The reunion, when it finally came, was happy but restrained. Charlotte was looking well, expecting her third confinement.

Mr. Collins's girth had also waxed, in consequence of his fondness for good dinners and teas. Elizabeth was amused to observe his evident hesitation and confusion in greeting her: should he flatter and fawn over the wife of Mr. Darcy of Pemberley, or should he still speak to her as he had always spoken to his lowly female cousin?

Many awkward pauses and many glances across to Lady Catherine to study the line that she took passed before Mr. Collins could resume some measure of composure. Elizabeth's own reflections and amusement—which she took care to conceal—were her only solace for the necessity of deferring an uninterrupted chat with her friend Charlotte.

The dinner produced nothing new by way of conversation save for the news that Mrs. Jenkinson was to spend the holidays with one of her nieces and would leave on the morrow.

Elizabeth was able to wish Mrs. Jenkinson a pleasant journey with more than polite cheerfulness, for it was difficult to approach Anne when her companion was ever by her side. Mrs. Jenkinson was zealous in the discharge of her duties, especially when Lady Catherine was within hearing—constantly enquiring as to whether Anne was too hot or too cold, or wanted the fire-screen moved, or needed a footstool, or more tea. She answered questions on Anne's behalf, counted her cards for her, and was at pains to spare her from any mental or physical exertion whatsoever. The lady's absence was an unmixed blessing, as far as Elizabeth was concerned.

Of course, Elizabeth's chief occupation was to attend her hostess every day, listening to her remarks, advice, and warnings. It fell to

Elizabeth's lot, just as naturally as it was the privilege of her husband and Colonel Fitzwilliam to spend most of their daylight hours out of doors walking or riding as they made a tour of the park with Her Ladyship's steward. When they returned, they were at the billiard table or in the library. Elizabeth spent no less than four hours in conversation with her hostess where her husband spent one—a sacrifice that was richly rewarded when baby Catherine, placed upon Her Ladyship's lap, promptly burped and deposited her breakfast on the lady's fine brocade gown.

The days leading up to Christmas might have blended into a sameness for Elizabeth, a fortnight with much to be tolerated and little to be enjoyed, had it not been for the slow, cautious, but definite progress of her friendship with Anne. .

"Have you noticed, my dear, that every time Anne says something, her mother demands 'what are you speaking of,' and then takes the conversation into her own hands?" Elizabeth asked her husband as she sat brushing her hair one morning about a week into their visit.

"That would explain why Anne speaks so seldom," mused Darcy, bending down to kiss the top of his wife's head. "She spares herself the vexation of being interrupted."

"Poor Anne!" Elizabeth continued. "Lady Catherine is forever speaking of 'Anne's indifferent health' and what she might have accomplished but for her delicate constitution."

"Can I ever thank you enough, my dear, for your patience and forbearance with my aunt?"

"I doubt you can." Elizabeth laughed. "Or rather, I shall collect the debt with interest when we are home again at last in Pemberley!"

Elizabeth did not add that she had observed Anne carefully but saw no symptoms of a broken heart. Elizabeth's heart still sang whenever her husband walked in to the room; she believed she would perceive it if so strong a sentiment stirred in Anne's breast. Anne was but distantly cordial to Darcy.

As she hoped, Elizabeth's stratagem of talking about books had helped to overcome Anne's reserve. She produced a new volume every day—a novel or a travel book—with a friendly enquiry: "Have you read this one, Cousin Anne? This contains the most enchanting descriptions of Italian scenery" or "This novel is rather silly, but I confess that I enjoyed it greatly. Have you read it?"

Elizabeth was now greeted with shy smiles and, while Anne never shared any information about herself and seldom gave an opinion about anything, she did display, in her quiet comments to Elizabeth, a knowledge of the finest poets and playwrights of the past century as well as the best-known works on history.

"Are you and my daughter speaking of books again?" demanded Lady Catherine on Christmas Eve as the family gathered in the drawing room after dinner.

"This is the season for indoor pleasures such as a good book, is it not, Your Ladyship?" answered Elizabeth respectfully.

"Yes, but everything should have its due proportion. It is essential that a lady have an education, but it is most undesirable that she should display her learning and be thought a pedant. It will not do at all. It is most unbecoming and unrefined. Will you play for us instead, Mrs. Darcy?"

"Certainly, Your Ladyship."

Lady Catherine was unusually attentive when Elizabeth took her seat at the pianoforte and began to play the pastoral music from Handel's *Messiah*.

A handsome fire burned in the hearth, and clusters of candles cast soft pools of light around the room. Through the multi-paned windows, which stretched almost from the floor and high overhead to the ceiling, the large, fat lazy flakes of snow glistened against a sky as black as ink. A feeling of tranquility filled the room as Elizabeth's music spoke of "peace on earth, good will toward men."

Darcy's eyes met those of his wife for a moment and they exchanged a heartfelt glance, he silently thanking her again, and she reassuring him with her smile that she did it all for love of him.

The nursemaids brought Darcy and Elizabeth's children for a visit before bedtime. Elizabeth had arranged that Lady Catherine should be the one to give the children their presents on Christmas Eve: a coral teething-ring for baby Catherine and Mr. Montgomery's picture book for William.

Neither child was inclined to linger long next to their benefactress. William promptly ran to his father, clutching his book, while Colonel Fitzwilliam took the baby so that Elizabeth might continue playing Handel and fill the room with the sound of angel's wings and celestial voices.

Anne quietly slipped out of her seat by the fire and joined Elizabeth at the piano bench.

"What a lovely sight," Anne whispered to Elizabeth. "Your husband reading to little William. Your little boy looks so engrossed! And so happy to be sitting with his father! I cannot remember much of my own father, but I do recall he used to read *Aesop's Fables* to me."

"My father never read to us," said Elizabeth, "but Jane and I were sometimes permitted into his study as a special treat. We were allowed to choose one of the books from his shelves and sit by the fire and read quietly. It was so peaceful, especially on a winter's night like this."

"I was quite a fanciful child," said Anne. "When I walked into our library and looked up at all of the volumes lining the shelves, towering above my head, I used to imagine the books whispering to each other, all in different voices. But books sit silently. They often sit unopened for years, waiting for you to open their pages so that they may begin to speak to you."

"Yes, and some book you had passed over a hundred times might, once it is allowed to tell its story, entirely enchant you so you cannot put it down, even if you had put off opening it many times before," said Elizabeth.

"What is that you are saying, Mrs. Darcy? What is it you are talking of?" came the familiar demand.

This time, it was Anne who answered.

"Happiness, madam. We were speaking of happiness."

ON CHRISTMAS MORNING, Elizabeth stood by one of the large, handsome windows overlooking the great lawn, holding baby Catherine in her arms. Outside, Darcy and William were building a snowman and marring the perfect expanse of sparkling white snow with their footprints. She suspected Lady Catherine would have something to say about that.

Elizabeth hoped the roads would be passable after Christmas. After almost a month away from Pemberley, she was longing for home again.

She became aware of Anne standing beside her, watching the scene.

"How I have enjoyed this Christmas season, Cousin Elizabeth. It has inspired me."

"Inspired you?" Elizabeth wondered at her choice of words, and Anne blushed.

"Seeing your children and watching them play. You see, I have a past-time—will you come with me for a moment to my bedchamber?"

Consumed with curiosity but delighting in this evidence of growing intimacy, Elizabeth carried the baby and followed Anne up the grand staircase to her apartment.

Anne's bedchamber was a surprise. Her walls were adorned with a few needlepoint samplers from her childhood. Nothing else. There was a narrow bed, no doubt the same bed she had used since she was a little girl. Elizabeth supposed that Lady Catherine—who still dictated when her daughter might leave the house or where she might go—was unwilling to admit that Anne was no longer a child.

A small dresser covered with bottles of tonics and medicines spoke of a lifetime of poor health and zealous doctoring. Elizabeth suspected that the latter had contributed to the former. There was a modest bookcase and a large old-fashioned wardrobe. A little table and two straight-backed chairs by the window commanded a fine view of the woods and, beyond that, the church spire in Hunsford.

Anne gestured out the window. "When I was a child, I longed to travel, to escape Rosings," said Anne. "True, it is very beautiful here. But I was lonely."

"You poor dear! Having four sisters, I really cannot imagine having so much solitude. How oppressive! But you saw your cousins now and again, did you not?"

Anne nodded. "Yes, and, of course, as soon I was old enough to comprehend, my mother began hinting to me that Fitzwilliam was to be my future husband. Perhaps if she had held her tongue, perhaps if she had not insisted upon it…who knows? I might have developed some kind of romantic feelings for him. As it was, though"—she shrugged—"I have imagined what a husband might be, and my imagination never painted anyone like my cousin." She added quickly, "Pray, do not think I am disparaging Fitzwilliam! He is in every respect a fine man and, when he was a boy, he was always kind to me.

Elizabeth nodded, pleased to have this glimpse of her husband as a boy and especially happy to hear from Anne's own lips that only Lady Catherine regretted the alliance that never came to be.

"So, with no one to talk with much of the time, I resorted to making up my own imaginary companions and writing little stories to amuse myself."

Anne pulled a chain from around her neck on which hung a small key. She opened a locked drawer in the dresser and revealed a bundle of papers.

At first Elizabeth assumed it was a diary. But Anne placed them on the small table and, moving closer, Elizabeth saw that that they were booklets made of folded-up paper and hand-stitched binding. The booklets were covered with writing in a small, feminine hand. Elizabeth picked up one of the booklets and started to read it.

The baby, sitting on her hip, began to wiggle and fret. Anne surprised Elizabeth by taking Catherine in her arms and cooing softly.

It was a story, a fairy story, about a child princess who lived in a castle on a mountaintop. From the very first pages, Elizabeth was caught up in the simple and charming tale. The princess could only leave the mountaintop in her dreams. When dreaming, she had a variety of adventures, only to wake up every morning in her bed.

Elizabeth sat in a chair by the fire and devoured page after page, losing herself in the tale. A bubble of laughter drew her attention to the sight of her daughter and Anne playing peek-a-boo with the window curtains.

"Anne? Can it be? Are *you* the authoress of this charming story?"

Anne blushed and looked away as though she wanted to hide

behind the curtains with the baby. "Yes. It is dreadfully childish. You must think me quite silly."

"No, no! This is wonderful! Wonderfully childish! That is to say, it has all the enchantment of childhood! You have invented an entire magical world. I would love to tell this story to my children when they are old enough to hear it. May I write out a copy?"

Pride was swiftly replaced with alarm. "Oh no! No, they mustn't leave this room! You are the only person to whom I have shown them!"

Elizabeth rose and went to place a reassuring hand on Anne's arm. "I promise you, I will not betray your confidence. But...do you have more stories like this?"

Anne nodded. "A great many, in fact. Some poems as well, although I do not think they are very good."

"I shall not importune you. But I cannot resist expressing my heartfelt conviction that your stories deserve to be shared with a wider world."

Elizabeth had a great deal more to say in praise of her cousin's writing, but Anne looked conscious and discomfited, as though she regretted her impulsive gesture in sharing her secret.

Elizabeth reluctantly dropped the subject and joined the game of peek-a-boo.

CHRISTMAS DINNER BROUGHT A DOZEN GUESTS. They included notable persons in the neighbourhood, Lady Catherine's steward, and, of course, the Collinses. Elizabeth was resigned to being placed as far as possible from the persons with whom she might have enjoyed speaking, having Mr. Collins for a dinner companion instead.

She had managed to pass more than a fortnight at Rosings without being pert or impatient with Lady Catherine. Her sacrifice would soon be at an end.

Although Lady Catherine had her faults, no one could deny the magnificence of her Christmas hospitality. Rich damask table linens set with crystal glasses and gold-plated china, extravagant candelabras, and arrangements of fruit and hot house flowers decorated the long banquet table in such profusion that one could hardly see the person opposite. The dishes, in gleaming silver, were served by a parade of footmen, in wave after wave. There were venison and beef roasts and turkey and goose and ragouts and soups and all manner of hothouse vegetables, puddings, jellies, and trifles in abundance.

All of Her Ladyship's guests made themselves as merry as possible and did justice to the meal laid before them. As for Elizabeth, she had only to listen as Mr. Collins entertained her during dinner with the minute details of his life and duties at Hunsford.

"Lady Catherine always orders her carriage for us when we return home, as you know, Mrs. Darcy, but on this occasion, on account of the snow and my dear Charlotte's condition, the carriage was sent to convey us here! Have you ever heard of such consideration and condescension?"

"I have not, Mr. Collins, and I am particularly glad of it for Charlotte's sake."

"Yes, and, were it not for Charlotte's wish that I keep her company, I would have stayed with my usual practise of walking up to Rosings. The distance is a trifle, and I have always held that daily walking is essential, not only for one's health, but for stimulating the intellectual powers."

"Indeed."

"The composition of sermons, especially when one has a patron so distinguished and cultivated as Lady Catherine de Bourgh..."

Alas, the rest of what Mr. Collins had to say on that topic was lost to oblivion. Try as she might, Elizabeth could not keep her mind from wandering, confident that she need only say "indeed" and "yes" at intervals. She found herself thinking again of Anne, who was seated next to Colonel Fitzwilliam at the table and appeared to be in excellent spirits.

I have behaved in an exemplary fashion during our visit, if I do say so myself. Would it be an inexcusable act of rebellion if I encourage Anne to find her voice, to share her talent with the world? No, I cannot think that I would be doing wrong. She is like the princess in the tower, and I could help to set her free....

The incessant drone in her ear continued, and she returned her attention to Mr. Collins in time to hear him say "...in fact, Mrs. Darcy, I have made a point of going for long walks in addition to working in my garden. And every Tuesday I walk three miles to Westerham, to visit with my fellow clerics, and back again, and I seldom take my pony cart, only if it rains, or is threatening to rain, or if the weather promises to be unseasonably hot, or cold, or windy."

"Indeed sir, you must not risk your health."

"My dear Charlotte says the same, but she encourages me to pause from my labours. 'You mustn't overtax yourself and spend the day in your study,' she always says. She makes a point of walking out every morning, and I go every afternoon. We are so alike in our thinking, you see. And what is more—"

"Which reminds me, Mr. Collins, I want to tell you that Mr. Darcy and I very enjoyed your sermon this morning, as Lady Catherine did not think it wise to venture out in this weather."

"And when you consider the benevolence of my patroness, Mrs. Darcy, you will understand why my topic for this Christmas was that we must always count our blessings."

Elizabeth glanced down the table where her husband was cordially making conversation with his aunt's guests. Two more nights, and they would bid farewell to Rosings! *There* was a blessing, indeed!

"Oh yes, Mr. Collins, indeed, a lovely sentiment for Christmas. We must count our blessings. I shall, whenever I think of you."

THE DAY AFTER BOXING DAY, the servants set about packing Elizabeth and Darcy's trunks for the journey which would take them back to London and finally home to Pemberley.

Elizabeth was in her bedchamber locking up her jewellery case. She wondered if she dared to plead with Anne one more time to allow her to have a copy of her manuscripts when there came a soft tap at the door...and there stood Anne with a small satchel.

"Elizabeth... I... I was wondering if...that is..."

"Yes, my dear, what is it? Come in—may I do anything for you?"

"I have been thinking about what you said and, if you do not think it is too silly of me, I should like it if you would take a copy of my stories with you when you go, and perhaps find someone who might like to publish them."

Anne held out the satchel, which Elizabeth took more reverently than the jewels she had just locked away.

"I feel very foolish—please, if no one wants to publish my stories, I shall not be at all surprised or put out. But you were so kind as to say—"

"I do say it, Anne. Your stories are delightful. I longed to urge you to do this, but I did not wish to be overbearing. Heaven knows, you have enough people in your life telling you what you ought to do!"

"This is my own decision, Elizabeth. I was thinking about it almost all night." Anne's voice had now dropped so low that Elizabeth had to strain to hear her. "I do not expect to marry, or to live a long life. Sometimes I think I do not mind it. Especially on a peaceful, snowy day like this, I could imagine that I might fall asleep and never wake up and be laid to rest in the family tomb next to father."

Before Elizabeth could protest, Anne went on:

"But if my stories could speak for me, then—that would be something of me that would last. It does not matter to me if I am known as the author. The opposite, in fact. I would like to send them into the world on their own merits without the name of 'de Bourgh' attached to them. I very much like to imagine that one day some mother or father will read my stories to their children. I shall be there, do you see? I shall be a part of those special memories between a parent and a child, those memories that last for a lifetime. How could I ask for anything more wonderful?"

There was a moment's silence, while Elizabeth wiped the tears that threatened to spill from her eyes.

"Anne, I shall be proud to do this for you. I promise, I shall write to you and let you know of my success."

Anne sighed, then shook her head. "Mother insists that I read my letters aloud to her."

Elizabeth acknowledged the difficulty, then ventured to say, "May I bring Mrs. Collins into our little confederacy? What if I were to correspond with her and tell *her* of my progress in getting your stories into print? And suppose I only told her of 'our mutual friend, the writer'? I will mention no names."

Anne flushed. "'The writer!' To think of myself as such! How presumptuous—yet how thrilling."

"I do believe we could contrive to do this. Charlotte could share the information with you, for I know you visit her. But do you never go to the parsonage without Mrs. Jenkinson?"

"Mrs. Jenkinson never gets out of the carriage. She is very rheumatic, you know. Half of the medicine in my bedchamber is hers! She does not want my mother to know how poorly she is for fear of losing her position."

"Oh, the poor dear. Our scheme ought to work, then."

Anne looked doubtful. "Is it wrong for me to involve other persons in my deceit?"

"Alas, we cannot consult Mr. Collins on this grave moral question, now can we?" Elizabeth laughed.

"Would Mrs. Collins object to keeping the secret from her husband?"

"Trust me, Anne. Mrs. Collins does not confide her every thought to her husband."

"And Fitzwilliam! Elizabeth, would you mind dreadfully, if... I should feel so foolish if no one wishes to publish my stories, or worse, what if they are published and no one buys them? Would you mind keeping our secret for the time being?"

"Of course, I will, if you wish it. But you have nothing to fear, particularly not from Darcy. I confidently predict that next Christmas, I will give Darcy a copy of your book, and it will say, "by a Lady" on the title page, and I will tell him who wrote it, and he will be tremendously proud of you! In the meantime, it is a delicious secret to hug to ourselves."

The resolve taken, not another word on the matter was exchanged. The ladies resumed speaking of indifferent subjects, but Elizabeth thought she detected a faint glow in the lady's pale cheeks when the Collinses arrived for a last dinner together before she, Darcy, and the children left for London on the morrow.

. . .

WHEN SHE FIRST BECAME A BRIDE, Elizabeth Darcy would have protested against the idea that a wife should ever keep anything remotely secret from her husband. As a married woman, however, and as the bearer of someone else's secret, she had to acknowledge that there were times, places, and circumstances which allowed of certain exceptions.

Therefore, when she left their London townhome in early January to make some morning calls, Elizabeth did not mention to her husband that she planned to call at the establishment of James Montgomery, publisher of children's books. Mr. Montgomery's establishment, in the days after Christmas, was quiet; the proprietor was in and fortunately at liberty to wait upon Mrs. Darcy.

Mr. Montgomery recognized his visitor instantly and ushered her into his office. Seeing his affable expression, Elizabeth felt confident that she was applying to the right person. At the mention, however, of "manuscript" and "fairy tales" and "by a lady," Mr. Montgomery sat back in his chair and assumed an expression of polite interest mixed with resignation.

"If you have no objection, Mrs. Darcy," he said, "I shall briefly inspect the manuscript now rather than undertaking to read the entire work. I should not like to raise expectations which I may later be compelled to disappoint."

"By all means, Mr. Montgomery," said Elizabeth evenly, unlatching the satchel and pulling out one of Anne's little booklets to hand to him. He took it with ceremonious politeness, and "begged her pardon, but he would read it now," while she waited, and "would she care for some tea?"

Elizabeth surmised that publishers were besieged by hopeful authors day and night and were forced to read through reams of execrable poetry and lurid melodramas. She was almost as anxious as though it was her own writing being judged, musing ruefully that Anne was fortunate in being miles away at Hunsford!

After Mr. Montgomery turned the first page, Elizabeth thought she saw a gleam of interest in his eye. She watched, scarcely daring to breathe, as he read two, three, four pages with unbroken concentration, not lifting his eye from the manuscript.

No, she was not mistaken! The story was pulling him in, just as it had captured her.

Three quarters of an hour went by, then James Montgomery suddenly looked up and said, "Mrs. Darcy, you have brought me something exceptional!"

"I knew it!" Elizabeth smiled. "My pleasure for my friend is seconded only by my delight in your confirmation of my good judgement."

"This *is* extraordinary, Mrs. Darcy," said Mr. Montgomery. "The tale is written for children, that is, it is a fairy tale—but there is a vividness of detail, a talent for delineating character, and a simplicity and beauty of dialogue that I have never encountered in a children's book before. I shall be only too pleased to publish it, and I have no doubt of its being an enormous success. You say that the authoress wishes to remain anonymous?"

"Oh yes, most definitely."

"But—I should very much like to meet her. Do I, in fact, have the honour of speaking with her at present?

Elizabeth laughed. "No, I am not your secret authoress. Let us call her 'Miss DB' for the present. For you see, she does not wish her closest relations to know that she intends to publish. I may as well tell you that she is very retired from the world and lives with her mother, a lady with the most strict and unbending views. *She* would be horrified if she knew what we were about."

"We must have some way of communicating, even if through a third party," explained Mr. Montgomery. "We must sign a contract, she and I. Then, once I have set up the book, there are galley proofs to be corrected—and I think we must find an illustrator to add at least a frontispiece."

"I offered to act as her agent but, as it happens, I shall be leaving London shortly. I had not thought of contracts and corrections and illustrations and so forth. But you may contact her, care of a mutual friend."

Mr. Montgomery nodded and then looked down again at the

manuscript in his hands. "I should very much like to meet her," he repeated. "I stopped believing in fairy tales a long time ago, but Miss DB might make me a believer yet again."

ELIZABETH RETURNED HOME in silent triumph, glowing with pleasure. All thoughts of morning calls were abandoned—empty conversation would not do—nor could Elizabeth call upon her Aunt Gardiner or her sister Jane for fear that she would succumb and share the delicious news. She found some vent for her feelings in writing and dispatching a letter to Mrs. C. Collins, the Parsonage, Hunsford.

She passed the rest of the afternoon with the children in the nursery, which is where Darcy, returning home, found her.

He paused at the doorway, silently appreciating the scene. Elizabeth was seated on a loveseat by the window with both children on her lap looking at the picture book. Catherine cooed and tried to grab the pages while William repeated, "H! Is for *horse*. H! Is for *horse*," with the serious mien of a child who realizes he is on the verge of sharing one of the world's great secrets.

Feelings of pride, love, and protectiveness, all welled up in Darcy. He wanted to stay there in the doorway and watch. He wanted the moment to last forever. He also wanted to take his wife in his arms.

He wanted to tell her he knew she had been hiding something from him—he had observed some furtive final whispers as she parted from Anne—the old leather satchel in the luggage—her unusual eagerness to summon the carriage, the driver and the groomsmen to make a social call that morning.

Whatever it was, he trusted her. He trusted her absolutely.

At last, she noticed him, and looked up and smiled. "Welcome home, Mr. Darcy."

You are looking exceedingly pleased with yourself, Elizabeth I think you no longer have any guilty secrets weighing on your conscience."

"Guilty secrets?" Elizabeth looked startled.

"Did you not say how much you regretted your secret disapprobation of cousin Anne? And did you not befriend her?"

"Oh! Oh, yes, that. There is nothing like knowing one has done the right thing."

Darcy smiled. "I always trust you, Elizabeth, to do the right thing. And perhaps one day you might enjoy telling me about it."

"Yes, I will, my dearest."

LONA MANNING is the author of the novels *A Contrary Wind* and *A Marriage of Attachment*, both based on Jane Austen's *Mansfield Park*. She has also written numerous true crime articles, which are available at www.crimemagazine.com. She has worked as a non-profit administrator, a vocational instructor, a market researcher, and a speechwriter for politicians. She currently teaches English as a second language and spent four years teaching in China. You can follow Lona at lonamanning.ca where she writes about China and Jane Austen.

HOMESPUN FOR THE HOLIDAYS

J. MARIE CROFT

We all know him to be a proud, unpleasant sort of man; but this would be nothing if you really liked him. —Jane Austen

PART 1: WHAT THE DICKENS?

*T*ension building in neck and shoulders, F. William Darcy switched the controls to snow mode as the temperature dropped sub-zero and intermittent rain turned to snow. *Brilliant! As if adjusting to driving on the right side—wrong side!—of the road wasn't bad enough.*

He decelerated, begrudging the loss of precious time.

The past week had been nothing short of abysmal. *Sorting out the Wickham cock-up, socialising at the office party, being dragged around by Bingley, forced to socialise with underlings, and having to dance with Caroline.*

Shuddering, he turned up the heat. Gripping the leather steering wheel, he ran through his agenda once again.

Leave boutique by four, jumper in hand. Head to airport, drop off rental. Board and sleep en route. Land—white-knuckled—and locate James and the Bentley. Arrive in London, knackered. Rush up to penthouse, don gay apparel

(charcoal suit, red tie, fake smile), and—"dashing through the"...fog—make my way to Mayfair. Spend what little will be left of Christmas Day with dear Georgiana...plus four spoiled kids, three insufferable cousins, two meddling aunts, one barmy uncle, and a taxidermic partridge in a blooming pear tree from Matlock's bloody orangery. Bah, humbug!

After hours on I-95 North, the navigation system in the hired Discovery Sport informed him to take the next ramp. "It's called a slip road, not a ramp," he mumbled, strained to his limit and headachy.

Someone—and he highly suspected who—had sabotaged the Land Rover's InControl apparatus. Instead of the accustomed dulcet English tones, the SatNav system spoke in an American twang similar to the young female who had answered—*after seven bloody rings!*—the phone at Homespun, his next and last stop for Christmas shopping.

At his command, the satellite radio came to life. From the Meridian sound system, instead of the expected strains of classical music, "Grandma Got Run Over by a Reindeer" blared through its seventeen speakers. Wincing and cursing, he stabbed at the touch-screen, switching from one pre-set country station to another. "Aargh!" In no mood for his friend's shenanigans, he hit mute. "Bingley, I'm going to kill you, you wanker!"

Exiting the motorway and bypassing the more populous town of Longbourn, William squinted through driving snow at a sign welcoming him to "Merryton, population 6,500." Some optimistic graffiti artist had incorporated the extra *R* into the town's name.

He turned, as directed, onto a winding road surrounded by bucolic hobby farms and tasteful but, to him, modest houses, all decorated for the holidays. Glancing around, he did a double take. *What the...?* Each and every property had the same tacky, inflatable, waving Santa on its front lawn.

Halfway down the road, the SatNav, in its annoying twang, announced his destination. *Strange. No signage indicates such, but that farmhouse on the left must be the place.*

All manner of vehicle—Subarus, pickup trucks, people movers— lined the driveway plus both sides of the road. Parking at the end of the line, he donned his cashmere hat and Pickett wool-lined gloves, pulled up the collar of his luxurious Zilli coat, and walked nine car lengths along the snow-covered gravel shoulder, cursing his inadequate footwear (hand-sewn Dover derbies with double leather soles, tanned for nine months in a solution of oak, spruce, and mimosa bark). Although unequalled in comfort and durability, the smooth-soled shoes did little to prevent his slipping, sliding, and uttering oaths about the weather in "New" England. *What's wrong with jolly "old" England? Couldn't Georgie have found a jumper there?*

A middle-aged couple—clad in apparel straight from L.L. Bean, which Bingley favoured for weekend wear—approached, nodding and smiling their hellos.

"Pardon me," said William, "but where's the Homespun boutique?"

The puzzled woman peered at him while snow accumulated on her woollen hat. "Boutique?"

Pushing up his cuff, William glanced at his Pinion wristwatch with dual time-zones. *Damn! Already behind schedule.*

"Yes, a small shop selling fashionable clothes and accessories. Do you know its whereabouts?"

Directed to a red-roofed outbuilding next to the house, William slipped and slid his way past smiling folk toting kraft bags.

What sort of upmarket business occupies a barn and uses plain paper sacks? Even Pottery Barn isn't an actual barn... Is it? And for that matter, what sort of business doesn't offer online shopping?

Fairy lights adorned the yard's snow-covered pines. Chickadees flitted about the branches and clung acrobatically to mesh bags filled with suet. If not for the incongruous resident inflatable Santa, the scene might have resembled a greeting card.

Snow creaking underfoot and distant strains of "Let it Snow" reaching his ears, William nodded at other shoppers as they passed and wished him a merry Christmas. *"Every idiot who goes about with merry Christmas on his lips should be boiled with his own pudding and..."* something, something, something. I really must re-read Dickens.

A cedar wreath with red berries and pinecones adorned the barn door, and a bell above it jingled as he stepped inside. Hand still gripping the handle, he froze.

What the hell? Instead of the upscale shop he expected, the place resembled a craft fair, complete with jumble table.

"Come in, come in! And close the door! Were you born in a barn?" A teenager in black leggings, Timberland boots, oversized, pillar-box-red sweater and matching nail varnish laughed and grabbed his sleeve, pulling him inside. The embroidered patch on the front of her sweater said "Pole Dancing" and had cartoon elves capering around the North Pole. "Brr! It's cold enough to freeze your Winnebago out there!"

"I beg your pardon?"

"Hi! I'm Lydia Bennet. Welcome to Homespun. Would you like to browse, or," she purred, "is there something in particular *I* could show you?"

William slipped off his gloves and reached inside his coat. "My sister saw this item on Instagram." He scrolled through photos on his mobile before turning the screen her way. "I called ahead and bespoke that particular jumper."

"Could you please speak English? What does *bespoke* mean? And that's one of our *sweaters*, not a jumper." Once he explained, Lydia shrugged. "Sorry. Mrs. Long came by earlier and bought that sweater for her niece."

"What?"

"I said, Mrs. Long came by—"

"Yes, I heard you the first time. But I told the girl on the phone I'd be by in a few hours to make the purchase. She assured me it would be held."

"You spoke with *me*, sir, but you hung up before I could ask your name and number."

William swiped away the photo and pocketed his mobile. "Do you not have another jumper just like that one?"

Lydia shook her head and beckoned a girl in an asparagus-green sweater with a huge appliqué on the front. Squinting, William discerned a cartoonish roll of festive, red wrapping paper sporting shades, bling, and holding a mic. He rolled his eyes. *Of course. Rapping paper, yo.*

Lydia led him over to the counter. "I'm sorry, but we don't hold items without a name and number."

"What sort of money-grubbing enterprise and shoddy service is this? I bespoke that item and intend to leave with it. The mistake was yours, and I expect you to rectify it." His strong jaw line became harder. "Get on the phone with whomever was given my jumper, explain the circumstances, and ask her to return it before I become properly browned off!"

"Is there a problem, Lyddie? May I be of assistance, sir? I'm Cathy Ben—"

Swinging round, William shouted, "Yes! This incompetent clerk sold *my* jump—sweater."

"Oh?" Lydia smirked. "Had you taken it off and put it down somewhere?"

"We recycle and felt old sweaters to make mittens," said Cathy, "but only *donated* ones are used in Liz's creations."

Elbow on counter, chin resting on hand, Lydia eyed William up and down. "Right. We haven't *yet* resorted to stealing customer's clothing off their backs."

He huffed. "Not *my* jumper! The one I bespoke over the phone. I was assured the item was in stock. But this *muppet*"—he pointed to Lydia—"sold it to another customer by mistake."

"He didn't provide, as per policy, the necessary info."

"Listen here. Either get on the blower and have *my* jumper fetched or produce another." Forefinger stabbing the countertop, William spoke sharply. "I demand satisfaction. I shan't go until you've given me the jumper I want. Do us all a favour, and bring one out here. Now! Off you go!"

Brilliant. I sound like either Aunt Catherine or the song they just played —in which wassailers won't leave until they get some figgy pudding. Damn.

More angry with himself than anyone else, he towered over the sisters. "Crack on, ladies, or I'll file a complaint with your manager. What are you waiting for? I have a flight to catch, and you prats are trying my patience."

Lydia's jaw dropped, and she gawped.

Cathy's lower lip trembled as she blinked away tears.

From behind William, a woman started singing. "You better watch out. You better not cry. Better not pout. I'm telling you why..."

William turned in amazement. A queue had formed behind him. The grey-haired woman, singing at the top of her lungs, was gradually joined by one after another of the shoppers in line. "...gonna find out who's naughty or nice. Santa Claus is coming to town."

Every person in the shop—with one notable exception—raised their voice in song. Every eye was directed at him as he stood, frozen, in front of the counter. "He knows when you've been bad or good. So be good for goodness sake!"

Accustomed to speaking in front of stern-faced directors in conservative boardrooms or boozy philanthropists at lavish banquets, F. William Darcy felt his face reddening as the song ended. *Criminy. I haven't blushed in donkey's years...if ever!*

Facing them, William realised their expressions spoke not of bad-temper but pity and embarrassment over his poor attitude. Duly ashamed, he remained frozen in place.

A group of teenage girls brushed past him to hug and console Cathy and Lydia.

Squaring his shoulders and inhaling deeply, William raised his chin. Fake smile in place, he nodded and applauded the carollers, then strode outdoors for a breath of fresh air, hoping to cool his heated cheeks.

It took less than a minute.

The weather had taken yet another turn for the worse. The late afternoon sky had grown black, and a gust of north-easterly wind swept tiny ice pellets and freezing rain across the snowy yard. A gritter—motor growling, blade scraping on gravel and pavement, flashing lights muted by swirling precipitation—spread salt along the opposite side of the road. Needle-like projectiles lashed William's face, forcing him to turn back just as a tide of anxious locals surged outward toward their vehicles and homes.

Confident in the Land Rover's ability to get him safely to the airport on time, William re-entered the shop. *Despite abominable customer service, something more than Georgie's obsession with a fluffy pink jumper impels me to linger.*

Brushing ice crystals from his coat and removing hat and gloves, he breathed in mingled aromas of evergreen, wood smoke, brewed coffee, spicy mulled cider, and baked goods. His stomach growled. *Ah, that's why I linger. I'm hangry.* Nothing more substantial than a handful of macadamia nuts—plus an inferior takeaway coffee—had been eaten since breakfast, and his inflight gourmet meal was still hours away.

Treading across creaky plank floors, he noted the barn's aged beams, antique wood stove, and seasonal decor he'd been (in his snit) oblivious to before. A massive balsam fir tree—with white lights and an eclectic assortment of handmade ornaments—occupied a corner. Around the room's perimeter, clotheslines were strung with patchwork quilts; woollen hats and socks; knitted scarves; crocheted baby blankets, bonnets, and booties; felted-wool mittens made from recycled sweaters; and, of course, the infamous sweaters themselves. Most items had embroidered appliqués with groan-inducing puns. William caught himself sniggering at a few and glanced around, hoping no one had noticed.

Few people remained in the shop.

Two middle-aged women, obviously siblings, stood behind a work table gathering up quilt blocks and reels of cotton, packing them into totes. Whispering, they looked his way until joined by a beautiful redhead with a coat draped over one arm.

Another reason to linger.

"Mom, did the Lucases say whether any of their relatives need the loft? I've cleaned the bathroom and changed the linens. It'll be warm and cosy up there as long as the stove keeps burning, and there's enough firewood stacked in the storeroom to last a week." Donning her coat, the redhead added, "I'm heading over now to help Dad with supper."

"The relatives are staying at the inn, but thanks for doing that, Jane. I didn't have the energy to deal with that wretched pull-down staircase today, not after cooking and baking all morning, then working out here. I'll drive Sis home and be back lickety-split." The woman speaking glanced at a frosted window while buttoning her coat. "I hope Ed and his family arrive soon. It's nightfall and not fit for man or beast out there." She beckoned her sister, and they followed the redhead out into the storm.

"Baby It's Cold Outside" blasted from the barn's speakers. William sang along in his head. *I really can't stay. Baby it's cold outside. I gotta go away. Baby it's cold ou—*

A cleaner holding a push broom had flipped a switch, silencing Idina Menzel and Michael Bublé.

I really "should" go. I still have a three-quarter-hour drive before me. But first, a flipping jumper to procure!

Employees were involved in the shop's closing routine—tidying up, turning off tree lights, sweeping the floor, counting cash at an old-fashioned till. "Pardon me," he addressed Cathy, "but I wonder if you've had a chance to retrieve my jumper."

The young women all dropped what they were doing to stare at him.

"Geez," cried Lydia, scrambling out from under the tree, extension cable in hand, "I thought you were long gone."

"As you see, not." William drummed his fingers on the counter. "So…?"

Cathy, gathering a wad of bills into her hand, heaved a sigh. "Dang! I lost count again."

Lydia brushed dust from the knees of her black leggings. "Truly, we assumed you had been driven away by— I mean, we thought you had driven away after, um, the, ah…"

"After the flash mob, you mean?" Darcy smirked. "No. We've still the matter of a jumper to settle."

The worker William had assumed was the caretaker emptied her dustpan into the bin, placed her push broom against the counter, and waltzed up to him, bold as brass. The embroidered, decorated evergreen and "Spruce Things Up" patch on her apron reinforced his presumption.

She extended her right hand. "Hello. I'm Elizabeth. May I be of assistance?"

Wrinkling his nose, William flinched away from her grimy palm. "I think not."

Exchanging cagey looks with Cathy, Lydia scooted behind the counter. Both girls leaned elbows on the polished wood and waited, chins propped on hands. "I wish we had popcorn," Lydia said.

William glared at them. "You've given me no option. I've run out of time and patience and must demand your manager be brought into this straight away." Twice, he snapped his fingers. "Fetch him for me."

"Him?" Elizabeth's smile didn't reach her eyes.

"Uh-oh!" cried Cathy at the same time Lydia shouted, "Take cover!" Together, they giggled.

Why must teenaged girls be so dappy? "I beg your pardon. You're entirely right. One shouldn't make assumptions about gender. Nevertheless, kindly ask your employer to join us."

Elizabeth bowed her head, all meekness. "Of course, sir. Right away, sir." Stepping to the far end of the counter, she untied her apron, flinging it on a chair. A young woman—wearing a black sweater with an appliquéd "Frostbite" and a vampire snowman—polished the wooden surface. Elizabeth winked and snatched the rag from her hand. "Thanks, Mary."

Wiping her hands on the waxy cloth, she walked back to the others. Tossing the grotty rag to the two girls, she extended her right hand to their customer. "Hello. I'm Elizabeth Bennet. While not technically the manager, I *am* in charge here. May I be of assistance?"

William's eyebrows shot up. *Should another of today's performances be applauded? No, no, best not. Those eyes shoot fire. Mustn't fan the flames. Instead of clapping, shake her hand, wanker.*

Long, strong fingers slid against daintier, waxier ones. Green, challenging eyes held fast to his darker ones. Clasping hands, they shook once—a firm, lingering, mutual squeeze until, as one, they discovered a hot potato in their grip and snatched back their hands.

Stone the crows! "Yes," he croaked before clearing his throat. "There's been, you see, a bit of a problem. Earlier today, I reserved one of your jumpers. But *someone*"—he glared at Lydia—"sold it out from under my nose."

Elizabeth asked if he had given his information.

Still speaking condescendingly but in a kinder tone than used with her younger sisters, he drew himself up. "No. I'm ex-directory and didn't want my name, F. William Darcy, bandied about." His eyes widened at her puzzled expression. "You haven't heard of me?"

"No, but I've heard plenty *about* you. Folks hereabouts spoke of little else following your outburst. The English gentlemen *I* know pride themselves on being comparatively civil."

He stiffened, head rearing up. "Say no more. I understand. I properly bodged that up." Yanking at the knot pressing on his Adam's apple, he gritted his teeth. "Sorry." Readjusting the tie, he forced a smile. "There now, let's put all this behind us, shall we? I'm in a hurry, so please be so kind as to fetch one of the 'Peas on Earth' jumpers from the back room, and I'll be on my way."

Rubbing wax from her palms onto her jeans, Elizabeth explained their wares were not mass produced. "We called our organisation 'Homespun' for a reason. Each item we sell is unique, lovingly crafted by local knitters, crocheters, quilters, and such."

"Yes, yes, I get it," he grumbled, still offended, still on the offensive. "Homespun, as in clothes made from fabric spun at home and, by extension, clothes that are plain and homely...like those worn by American colonists who boycotted British goods back in the day."

Hands on hips, Elizabeth stepped forward until her Columbia Bugaboots were toe-to-toe with William's shiny Edward Green shoes. "Do you find our merchandise lacking in any way?"

Glancing around, he shrugged. "Your merchandise is tolerable, I suppose, in a charming, amateurish sort of fashion. Admittedly, though, I have rather high standards and rarely shop off-the-peg. Items must be of impeccable quality to tempt *me*. But, for some reason, someone very dear to me simply must have that fluffy, pale pink 'Peas on Earth' jumper or she'll—in her words—*simply die*. How long would it take to make another? Fifteen minutes?"

"Make another!" Elizabeth spluttered. "Fifteen minutes! It takes our machine nearly fifteen minutes alone to complete that seven thousand-stitch embroidery design of green peas atop a globe. And that's not mentioning the time it takes to sew on the appliqué afterwards."

"How can it take a quarter hour to recreate a twee drawing?"

Mary huddled with her younger siblings. "Pray for peace."

Sotto voce, Lydia quoted, "Peace on Earth! Give me presents!"

Ignoring the others, William plucked from the clothesline a soft, shell pink sweater, thrusting it at Elizabeth. "It seems a simple enough process. Slap the appropriate embroidery on this bog-standard jumper and Bob's your uncle."

Her laughter had a decided edge. With sweeping arm gestures,

Elizabeth directed his attention to the items folded on shelves and hanging from the line. "For six months, friends and neighbours worked on these labours of love. Not for some pampered girlfriend of F. William Darcy, but for a sick child who might not live to see another Christmas unless she gets the costly medication she needs to survive. *That's* why we created Homespun—a not-for-profit organisation run by my family and supported by our volunteers."

Taking a deep breath, Elizabeth ran fingers through her hair, dislodging auburn locks from the clip holding her messy bun. "It's Christmas Eve. We're all looking forward to closing shop and being with loved ones."

"A worthy cause, I grant you, and I applaud your initiative. But, see here, there is such a thing as false advertising, and your—"

Sighing and shaking her head, Elizabeth gazed at the ceiling beams. "You don't get it. Other than photocopied flyers on a few community bulletin boards, we never advertised. The sick girl's sister —my best friend Charlotte—posted photos of our creations on Instagram, Pinterest, Twitter, and Facebook. The whole thing went viral without our knowledge...until we started getting thousands of inquiries."

"You had no marketing plan?"

"This was meant as a local fundraiser only, but it got out of hand. Imagine my surprise when the rich and famous decided our *charming* —your word, not mine—woollen goods should become the latest trend. So, here we are, hardly able to keep up with demand. We're ecstatic to have raised so much money for Mariah, but we're tired... and, I fear, emotional. I apologise on behalf of my sisters and myself."

Her explanation left Darcy gobsmacked. *I know all about working long, hard hours. About being tired and emotional.* He apologised for his behaviour, adding, "This time, I mean it."

Elizabeth raised her chin. Green eyes, luminous with tears, searched his own for sincerity. She offered him a wobbly smile, then some coffee, mulled cider, or candy-cane hot chocolate. "And there are a few cinnamon buns and gingerbread reindeer left on that trestle table...next to a stack of Dad's used books that nobody wants. Interested?"

William thanked Elizabeth, accepted a bun and a biscuit, and wolfed them down. "I really must be on my way, though. I have a flight to catch, and the roads are, most likely, treacherous."

"Haven't you heard? The worst ice storm in fifty years is approaching. State police just issued a warning that motorists should stay off the roads. Airports are telling travellers to check their flights online before heading out."

Flight Tracker already programmed in, William's mobile was at his ear in seconds. Gentleman that he was, he turned away so no one would hear any four-letter words if his flight was cancelled. His head and shoulders dropped, his eyes closed. *Oh, God. I'm so sorry, Georgiana. I've failed you again.*

He discovered the Bennet sisters watching his every move. As his eyes met theirs, they looked away, busying themselves. Mary switched off the coffee machine and urns of cider and hot chocolate. Cathy and Lydia wrapped leftover baked goods in clingfilm while their elder sister secured the deposit.

Elizabeth fetched outerwear from pegs behind the storage room door. Distributing them, she insisted her sisters go home. "I'll be along shortly. I heard car doors a while ago. Ed, Martha, and the kids must have arrived."

The teens bid William a "Merry Christmas" and headed for the exit. Struggling against a gale-force wind, Lydia grunted, pushing at the barn door.

"Here. Allow me." William put his shoulder to the heavy wood, forcing it outward. A blast of frigid air stole his breath. The door slammed behind him as he turned back into the room, shaking ice crystals from his hair. "Gad! It's cold enough to freeze the bal— Er, it's a bit parky out there this evening."

Elizabeth waited.

"Yes. Cancelled, as you must have surmised. *All* flights cancelled." Combing back his forelock with cold fingers, he forced another smile. "Now... Do you happen to know where I left my hat and gloves? And, more importantly, where I might find the nearest hotel?"

"Our nearest—our *only*—accommodation is a mile away. The Meryton Inn has just three rooms, all occupied by Lucas relatives here to visit Mariah over the holidays. Sorry. Unless you have friends nearby, you're stuck. My parents would offer to put you up for the night, I know they would, but our place is packed, too. We've four bedrooms, but my aunt, uncle, and four cousins are staying with us, as is Dad's cousin. By now, all beds, air mattresses, and pull-out sofas have been claimed, and— Wait! You can sleep *here,* in the barn. Up in the hayloft."

"What? Are you honestly telling me, on Christmas Eve, there's no room at the inn? And that I must sleep in a stable? In *hay?*" William guffawed then sobered, dragging hands down his face.

Elizabeth explained the loft had been converted into a studio apartment. "There's a double bed and a few other furnishings. And, of course, a bathroom. With shower. You'll just have to watch your head. You're so very...*tall* and..." A flush crept across her cheeks. "And the walls are all slanted. Except in the very middle, of course." Rubbing her brow, she looked away. "Sorry, I'm babbling."

William opened his mouth to accept, but his stomach spoke first.

"When's the last time you ate? Do you want another cinnamon—" Elizabeth slapped her forehead. "Ugh. Obviously not thinking clearly. Come over to the house, please. Join us for supper. There'll be enough food to feed an army or, at least, Bill. First, though, you should park your car in the yard. Our snow-plow driver gets riled when vehicles are on the shoulder."

He graciously accepted her offer. *I'm buggered. What choice do I have?*

After a search for William's hat and gloves, Elizabeth bundled herself in a hooded coat and mittens and wound a Homespun scarf around her neck. While she turned off the lights, he fought with the wind over control of the door.

Outside, squinting against the elements, she gripped his arm, helping William keep his impractically shod feet beneath him. Through ice-encrusted snow, they trudged to the SUV—where they stood for two minutes arguing about her scraping, or not scraping, the windshield.

"Be sensible. I'm wearing proper winter footwear. You're not."

He, indignant at such a suggestion, opened the passenger door and insisted she get in. She, lips pressed together, complied. William slammed the door, or the wind took it. Whichever force was to blame, he slipped and disappeared from her sight.

"Men!" She inched the door open, bumping the side of his head as he pulled himself up.

In the driver's seat, William pushed the starter and set the automatic climate control to max. Rubbing his head, he watched as an obstinate, mittened, aubergine anorak—for that was all he could see of Elizabeth—cleared ice from the windscreen with his anodised titanium credit card. "How was I to know there's no scraper?"

Along with the north-east wind, Elizabeth breezed in, shivering. "I'm so sorry!" At his blank expression, she added, "Dropped it. Just need a minute to thaw out. Then I'll go search again. Should be easy to spot against the snow."

"Dropped what?" *Don't say credit card. Please don't say you dropped my Black—*

"Your credit card."

"Blimey." Inch by inch, William bent forward until his forehead rested on the steering wheel, mumbling about needing petrol to make it to the airport and paracetamol to make it through the night.

A quarter hour later, Amex card secured in his breast pocket, he parked the Land Rover in front of the barn, and they slogged one hundred sixty yards to the front of the house. At the bottom of the steps—"Whoa!"—William's feet shot out from beneath him.

Elizabeth yanked him up by his sleeve, saving him from landing on his expensively-clad bottom. "Careful of the icy patch. And, um, I should also warn you against mentioning anything to Mom about your Centurion card."

"I hardly go about boasting of such things," he huffed. Treading the steps carefully, holding onto the wooden banister for dear life, he glanced her way. "But why not, may I ask?"

His question went unanswered as the farmhouse's exterior and interior lights blinked twice, then went out—as did the street lamps, the twinkling fairy lights in the pine trees, and all sources of electrical illumination as far as the eye, in poor visibility, could see.

Into the pitch-blackness, Elizabeth let out a wail. "Ohhh, fffuuudge!"

PART 2: A BENNET FAMILY CHRISTMAS VACATION STORY

Blinded when the front door flew open, William reared back. A middle-aged man—clad in parka, corduroy trousers, snow boots, and frown—appeared before him, battery-operated lantern in hand, ready to brave the elements.

"Lizzy! I was worried sick! Why didn't you answer your phone?"

"Sorry, Dad. The battery must have died in the cold. Speaking of which, can we please come in, out of it?"

The man stepped back, holding open the door.

Elizabeth and William stomped their feet and brushed snow and ice from their clothing onto the hallway mat. After hanging his outerwear on a nearby coatrack to dry and adding his shoes to a large collection of boots, William stood awkwardly, glancing alternately at her and at the thirteen people of various sizes, shapes, and ages— torches, lanterns, or candles in hand—who gawped back at him.

"Oh! Sorry! Dad, Mom, this is F. William Darcy. He was shopping here on his way to the airport and will be sleeping in the loft. William, my parents, Tom and Jenny Bennet."

Shaking their hands, William exchanged a few civilities with his hosts.

"And," said Elizabeth, "I believe you've already met most of my sisters. Except Jane, here."

So taken with the beauty in the barn, William accepted Jane's cool, extended hand and... *Nothing. No blistering heat. No intense, challenging locking of eyes. Nothing.*

Elizabeth's father introduced the Gardiners and their four young children. "And," he said, grimacing, "the hulking fellow breathing down my neck is Bill Collins, my sixth cousin, thrice removed. Removed, but, like a bad penny..."

Chortling, Bill slapped his cousin's back before shaking William's hand. "Actually, third cousin, twice removed. A pleasure, Will. I have, needless to say, heard of *you*. I don't like to brag, but your aunt Catherine subscribes to my YouTube channel and occasionally leaves a scathing comment. The dear lady is just kidding, of course." Puffing out his chest," he added, "We're, you see, LinkedIn. Have been for years. You might say we're friends, although she has yet to accept my Facebook request." Letting go of William's hand, he said he had heard many good things about him and how glad he was that they finally met. "In fact, you might be interested in my next venture. I have this idea for a TED Talk and—"

"And *nothing*," said Jenny. "Supper is almost ready." Stroking William's superfine sleeve, she bustled him down the hall. "We'll dine by candlelight. Even in a power outage, we're not completely in the dark." Scowling over her shoulder at her cousin-in-law, she whispered to William. "At least *most* of us aren't."

William admitted he could do with a good nosh up. "I haven't properly eaten since breakfast."

"Our old propane stove has a standing pilot flame, so even the oven works. Now, come along. You and Liz must be frozen. There's mulled cider and buttered rum heating over the hearth. Do you take brandy in your cider? Or would you prefer a spiked eggnog?" Without awaiting an answer, she prattled on, barely taking a breath. "We'll fix you up with some Anadama bread toasted over the fire and a nice bowl of clam chow*dah*. That's how you pronounce chowder in New England: chow*dah*. If you're a vegetarian like Liz, we have corn chow*dah*, followed by a roasted vegetable quiche. There'll be crab cakes with Harvard beets and, of course, lobster served with melted butter. You don't look like a mac 'n' cheese kind of man to me, but that's what the youngsters will eat."

Bill scurried to catch up. "A minute of your time, please, Will."

William surreptitiously wiped, with his hankie, at the palm that had shaken the soap dodger's hand.

Carrying a torch, Elizabeth spoke from behind. "His name is *William*, Bill, and I expect he might like to wash his hands before eating."

Perceptive woman. "Yes, thank you. Where's the loo?"

Bill offered to show William the way, but Elizabeth reminded him he had to help her father with the lobsters. Like an overgrown cock-roach, he scuttered off into the dark.

Dingy in the poor light of torches and candles, the Bennet home, nevertheless, smelled clean and Christmassy. Tantalising aromas made delicious promises to William's stomach, and he inhaled deeply. Amongst more welcoming ones, the unpleasant smell of a person's unwashed body lingered. "Interesting bloke, your cousin."

"*Distant* cousin. Unfortunately for us, not distant *enough*...or able to *keep* his distance." The beam of Elizabeth's torch dimmed perceptibly as they reached the guest washroom. "He's intimidated, I think, by Jane's beauty. He hits on me, instead."

"He does seem a bit of a thickie."

"Right." Elizabeth gave a short, mirthless laugh. "A man would *have* to be thick to choose me over Jane."

Damn! "That's not at all what I meant. If you'd like, I could—What's the American football term? Run interference. Pretend I'm madly in love with you."

"Ha! I doubt you're *that* proficient an actor, but I'll keep it in mind. Here, take the flashlight. I'll wait on that deacon's bench over there. Don't want you getting lost on your way to the dining room."

Having availed himself of all the loo's facilities, William glanced at his watch before pulling out his mobile. *Might as well—while afforded some privacy—check up on Georgie before it's too late over there.* He tapped on her image then drummed on the wall, waiting, as the wind howled and shook the windowpane.

"Will! We've been so worried! Are you en route? We heard there's a blizzard raging along the US north-east coast."

"I'm temporarily snowbound, although it's more of an ice storm now. And there's a power outage." William pictured her pout while she asked when they might expect him. "Sorry, Georgie. I'll not be home for the hols." Holding the phone away from his ear, he waited as she threw a wobbly. "Are you quite finished? The weather, you know, is beyond even *my* control. It's not as if I *want* to be here."

"Where are you? The airport?"

"I never made it that far. I'm staying overnight in the back of beyond. Rustic place. Inhabited by hobby farmers, cheeky crafters, dappy teenagers, and clutching mothers…not to mention Chrimbo Santas and distant cousins filled with air."

"William Darcy, have you been drinking?"

"Not *yet*. I am, however, knackered, hangry, and very sorry to disappoint you, luv. To top it all off, I'm to sleep in a bloody barn tonight, in a hayloft. Doubt I'll catch much kip. Wish I was there with you." William listened while his sister ranted and whinged. "You can get all mardy about it if you like, Georgiana, but—" He crooned into the phone, "You better watch out. You better not cry. Better not pout. I'm telling you why…"

"You *are* out of your box, aren't you?"

William argued he was sober as a judge.

Georgiana reminded him that some eighteenth-century tosspot ancestor—whose portrait graced Pemberley's gallery—had been in that profession. Speaking to someone in the background, she told whoever it was to hold his horses. "There's a nosy parker here beside me who's beside himself with curiosity. We'll FaceTime tomorrow, okay? Here's Rich. Ta-ta! Love you!"

"Love you more— No, no, not *you*, wanker!"

William asked after all his relatives and expressed his regrets. "So sorry"—*not sorry*—"to be missing all the jollification." *All the "samey-ness," all the back-biting, all the overindulgences of a Fitzwilliam Chrissie knees-up.* "You won't believe the nightmare before Christmas I'm having."

After Richard's initial probing questions were answered, William elaborated at length on his first impressions. "And," he continued ranting, "even the baby bonnets have infantile puns embroidered on them. What do you mean 'What's wrong with that?' And why do you keep asking about *her*? No, I have *not* mentioned Elizabeth at least a dozen times!" *Have I?* "She—of the grotty apron and tacky jumper—is of no interest to me. Absolutely not! I have no intention, now or ever, of chatting her up or cracking on to her." *Liar, liar, pants on fire, nose as long as a telephone wire!* "Nevertheless, Rich, she's a proper fit piece. Elizabeth's teal jumper had 'Christmas Cheer' plastered across the chest, complete with two white pom-poms positioned at strategic points. I think the name of a local competitive cheer group was there, too. A part of me wanted to rise up and shout, 'Rah!' Truth be told, man, you should see *all* the Bennet sisters. Five of them. All close in age. All as hot as hell and...hold on a sec. Bloody torch battery just went flat, and I'm in the dark. Might as well sign off and grope my way to the dining room. Give everyone—except your prat of a brother—my love and apologies. Cheers."

Fumbling in the dark, William opened the door, wincing at the glow from a lantern on the floor across the hall. Raising his eyes, he spotted Elizabeth, arms folded, leaning against the wall instead of down the hall where she said she'd be. "Hello. Waiting for the loo or simply eavesdropping?"

"As you see, I found another lantern. Hearing what I thought was tapping on the wall, I came to investigate. Imagine my surprise!" Stepping forward until her stockinged feet were toe-to-toe with his, she spat, "So, *that's* your opinion of us, of our hospitality?"

Without boots, she was a bit shorter than she'd been during their row in the barn, yet, to William, Elizabeth appeared even more imposing than before. *She certainly makes me feel small.*

"I invited you—without knowing you from Adam—to sleep in our loft. Yes, it once held hay, but it's now a cosy, ensuite bedroom. Then I invited you into my home, offering you shelter from the storm, warm food, and drink. Tonight will be a special time, a time for family traditions. Yet I was willing to share it with a complete stranger. And *this* is how you thank me! Honestly, after hearing that representation, you're the last person on earth I want to spend Christmas Eve with. But I've made my bed and now must lie on it."

She looked away, pressing a hand to her stomach. "I pity poor 'Georgie.' Not because the pampered princess won't get the pink sweater she wants but because she has such a *prat*—whatever that means!—for a boyfriend."

"What did I say that wasn't true? Meryton *is* remote. Your society *is* rustic—with its tiny farms, folksy handicrafts, and a hokey extra *R* on your welcoming sign. I suspect your town council ordered it. Such simplicity is, however, charming...although I *could* do without all those Homespun puns."

"*I'm* not responsible for those. Dad, the English lit teacher, is. Look, I know Mom can be a bit grasping, but you didn't have to—"

"Technically, she *did* clutch my arm. Your sisters *are* dappy, and your cousin *is* full of hot air. And you... Your apron and hands *were* grimy, and"—holding up his own palm, he forestalled her—"I admire your *hands-on*, shall we say, managerial skills."

"Thanks for the back-handed compliment. But what you said about my sisters and me..."

"Admittedly, some remarks bordered on inappropriateness. I apologise. I'm neither sexist nor, I hope, a prat who doesn't realise how grateful he should be for all you've done. Thank you, Elizabeth. Now, I'd be even more grateful if we could head to the dining room before I faint from lack of food. You might not have guessed, but I can get in a bit of a strop when I'm famished. But, first..." Stepping back, he extended his hand.

She eyed it with suspicion.

"I washed it!"

They clasped hands, mutually letting go after two seconds.

He snatched up her lantern with his left hand, flexing the fingers of his right while Elizabeth guided him along the hallway.

"By the way—not that *you'd* care one way or the other—Georgiana, the so-called pampered princess, is my sister, *not* a significant other. FYI. Just so you'd know, and...all that."

"Oh. Okay." Her hip bumped his. "I'll bear that in mind the next time I jump to a conclusion."

William thought he saw a flash of white teeth, but he couldn't be sure. His own smile faded as voices reached him from the front hall.

"Google it, Cat. Zilli. Made in France. Pure silk lining and— Hold the light closer! Um, pure Peruvian v-i-c-u-n-a wool."

"Got it. One of the world's rarest natural fibres and... Holy mother of pearl, Lyddie! $23,093.37 for a coat! Add that to the $2,408.37 for his cashmere hat and $1,504.60 for those shoes. That's way more than you and I, combined, make in a year. Who *is* this guy?"

"Google him!"

"I can't," Cathy wailed. "My data ran out, and my battery just died. Dang it all to heck! No WiFi. I can't afford more data, my juice pack is drained, and now my phone is dead. How long will this outage last? I'll *die* without internet."

"Not a problem," said William, making the two girls jump. "The SUV can charge up to eight devices at a time. It's also a WiFi hotspot. Just don't waste petrol unnecessarily."

Lydia squealed as he tossed her the key fob, lunging forward as if she might embrace him. William backed away, bumping into Elizabeth.

Turning to apologise, he shone the lantern in her direction. Face pale, one hand over her mouth, she backed away, eye wide, shaking her head.

"Come and get it," called Jenny.

Was it her sisters' snooping or my extravagance that disgusted her? Either way, Elizabeth is appalled because of me. Should I stay or should I go?

A moment later, William stood in the candlelit dining room, waiting for the ladies to be seated.

"Don't stand on formality, Son," said Tom, turning away from toasting Anadama bread over the fireplace embers. "Grab a seat. It's casual dining tonight. We don't bring out the fine china, good linens, and best manners until tomorrow."

Still, William waited until Elizabeth chose a chair. She wouldn't look his way, and he agonised over her behaviour and his available seating options. The decision was taken away from him when the other men situated themselves around the table. Bill had claimed the coveted seat beside Elizabeth.

Every place was taken, save for the one that, under more formal circumstances, would have been William's anyway—the chair to his hostess's right, leaving him almost as far from Elizabeth as the table could possibly divide them.

"We take turns getting up and serving. The lobster course is mine." Jovial smile in place, Ed Gardiner told William to jump in, if so inclined. Jabbing the air over his left shoulder, he added, "Kitchen's that way."

Criminy. With my luck, I'd dump chowdah into Elizabeth's lap.

That course was served instead by Martha Gardiner. "Clam or corn, William?"

With Elizabeth watching, he blurted, "Corn, please." *Damn. I meant clam.*

The chardonnay was smooth, the fare simple but tasty, and the conversation lively. Other than compliments on the rich but tender texture of the boiled lobster, its pristine white flesh, its mild flavour, and how easy it was to eat with a fork from the shell, William contributed little to the natter.

He watched Elizabeth, though, attending her every word and becoming more and more impressed by her intelligence, her lively spirit, her generosity. *And drawn in by her deep, green eyes. Blimey. Never before have I been so potty about someone.*

As with every family gathering, however, there just had to be a degree of petulance.

Seated in front of the fire and next to Elizabeth, Bill, sweating profusely, complained about the temperature.

"Well, you know what they say," Tom and Cathy muttered together. "If you can't stand the heat, get out of the farmhouse." Everyone familiar with the source chuckled while William and Bill frowned in confusion.

During crab cakes, quiche, and a lull in the conversation, Jenny turned to William. "And what is it you do for a living?"

Choking on a sip of chardonnay, he gasped, "I— I'm— I'm an MD."

"A doctor!"

Dabbing the corners of his mouth with a serviette, he glanced down the table at Bill. "No, not a doctor. Amongst other titles and responsibilities, I'm a managing director, an MD, which is equivalent to CEO over here."

"How modest of you, Will. Obviously, you take after your aunt Catherine—the very model of self-effacement." Looking around at the others, Bill shook his head. "Don't you read Forbes? Don't you know who your esteemed guest is? Haven't you heard of F. William Darcy or his conglomerate, the FWD Group? You have, sitting at your humble table, one of the wealthiest, most prestigious men in the world."

Scowling, William threw down his serviette. "Now, see here. That's hardly accurate."

"It's true. Your aunt Catherine says so." Bill stuffed half a crab cake into this mouth, speaking around it. "And Will's uncle is an earl! My dear cousins, even had Will not inherited an outrageous fortune from his parents, he'd still be a billionaire several times over. His business savvy in the worlds of finance, investment, and real estate is nothing short of legendary. What are you worth now, Will? Come on, tell us. You're among friends."

Scraping back her chair, Elizabeth stood, glaring down at her greasy relative. "You're out of line, Bill. Can't you see what an awkward position you've placed our guest in? The poor man is spending Christmas Eve with strangers, not friends. And though he wishes to be anyplace else but here, I will not allow him to be embarrassed in our home."

"Actually, Elizabeth, you're only half right." Gentleman that he was, William could not remain seated while a lady stood. Gaining his feet and with eyes fixed on her, he spoke in a clear, calm tone. "Yes, he's out of line, and, yes, I'm uncomfortable discussing my finances. Otherwise, you're wrong. At least, I *hope* I'm amongst friends. And, right now, there's no place I'd rather be than here with you. Er, that is, *all* of you... Well, with one exception." William glared at Bill.

Silence reigned until one of the little boys cried for his dessert.

"Ah! My favourite course," said William. "I volunteer to serve the afters, or pud, as we civilised people call it. Er, that is, if Elizabeth will help me find my way around the kitchen." Smiling as she nodded, he snatched a torch from the sideboard. "And what am I serving?" he asked, following her out.

"Guess."

"I hope it's not Jello, rice pudding, or baked apples. I'm in the mood for something decadent. Something sinful," he whispered, his breath teasing the back of her neck.

Stopping at the kitchen counter, she turned to face him. "Guess again."

"You're no fun. Hmm. This being New England, it's probably something maple-flavoured."

"What's wrong with maple?"

"Not sinful enough. Oh, dear god! Not fruitcake! I despise fruitcake. Please tell me it's not fruitcake, or mince pies...or Oreos."

"You're a snob, you know that, right?"

"Think of poor little whatshisname out there and how disappointed he'll be if I serve him fruitcake. Think of the little boy, Elizabeth. Think of the little boy."

She laughed, and his heart soared. *Her laughter does things to me. Things.* "Wait. Where are you going?"

Their dessert, he was informed, was sitting in an ice-filled cooler buried in snow on their back deck, and she needed her boots to fetch it. He argued *he* should go. She argued he'd just fall again.

Too late. I'm already falling for you.

Although he did nothing but dish it out into small glass bowls which he placed on a tray, carried into the dining room, and distributed, William beamed as his adopted family dug into the Ben & Jerry's festive flavoured ice cream. *Caramel, chocolate chunks, pieces of crunchy gingerbread. Sinful.*

With the exception of Bill—who retired to the pull-out sofa in Tom's den to sleep off his supper and his faux pax—they all shuffled to the living room, groaning, and sinking onto every available soft surface, even the thick woven rug covering the hardwood floor. In front of the crackling fire, a black Lab and a Maine Coon cat snuggled together.

Togetherness. William watched the two little girls help their younger brothers hang stockings from the mantle. *It's all about togetherness.*

"Look, William," said Jenny, pointing. "Jane and Liz's teddy-bear stockings. They've had them since they were Sophia and Emily's ages. Mary and Cat own the Homespun ones—'Snowmen are Flakey' and 'Mother Nature Always Snows Best.' The tacky, stockinged-leg-lamp one is Lydia's."

Grinning, William turned to Elizabeth, beside him on the love seat. "You still hang a stocking?" She nodded. "Well, do you know why Santa is so jolly?" She shook her head. "He knows where all the naughty girls live."

Rising from his easy chair, Tom claimed everyone's attention. "It's Christmas Eve, the tree is trimmed, and the stockings are hung. Time for the Bennet annual carol sing. Take it away, Mary. William, please join in."

He hadn't noticed the upright piano tucked in an alcove, but William joined the others at the instrument, wishing Georgiana was with him. *My happiness would be complete.* Asked to select the first two pieces, he chose "The Holly and the Ivy" and "O Tannenbaum." While others followed the English translation, he sang the latter song in German from memory.

At Jenny's request, "I'll be Home for Christmas" came next. Noticing William's faraway look as they sang, Elizabeth sidled up, touching his hand, giving it a squeeze, then letting go. He wrapped his hand around hers, squeezing back, holding on till the end.

Martha exchanged places with Mary, flexing fingers over the keys. "This song is for my four little scamps. 'Old Toy Trains' is a favourite in our family. Ed, come sing it to our children with me before they go to bed."

William didn't know the song, but something tugged at his heart-strings as he listened and watched the young family.

That! That's what I want. That's what I've been missing in my world of meetings, cynicism, and stuffiness. Without conscious thought, his eyes turned to where Elizabeth softly hummed along with her parents and sisters.

Finally, as Mary and her parents performed "Away in a Manger" and the children went about the room saying their goodnights, William felt a tug on his trousers.

The eldest boy peered up at him. "Are you Jesus?"

"I beg your pardon?"

"Are you Jesus?"

"Certainly not."

"But you have an Uncle Earl and I heard Aunt Jenny say that makes you as good as the Lord, and Mary said we should pray 'cause you might be Mariah's saviour, and there was no room at the inn so you're gonna stay in the barn and sleep in the hay. Are you Jesus?"

Elizabeth hurried over. "Silly goose is half asleep. Doesn't know what he's saying."

The boy pouted, hugging a cuddly toy. "Do too! I heard—"

"Reindeer prancing on the rooftop," said Elizabeth. "Best scurry off to bed! But first, let's see what Jane has on that plate."

"Look what I found!" Jane lowered a plateful of biscuits for the children to see." Shortbread Christmas cookies! With Jimmies! Save some for Santa, though."

William turned to Elizabeth. "Jimmies?"

"Sprinkles."

"Ah. Hundreds-and-thousands."

"Of calories, yes. What would Christmas be without them? If you prefer, Mary is bringing in bowls of cut-up apples, Cabot cheddar, kettle-cooked potato chips, peppermint bark, and mugs of hot buttered rum. Yum. Or you can have some of Dad's brandy."

"I'm still stuffed to the gills with chow*dah* and seafood," he groaned. Admiring her trim figure, he asked where she put all the food she packed away. "You haven't an ounce of fat on you...not that I was checking you out or anything."

While Lydia pranced around the room singing "Santa Baby," William told Elizabeth he should head to the barn.

"Okay. Dad went over twice to stoke the fire, so the loft should be comfy. Get bundled up while I fetch another duvet, just in case. Do you want to borrow a pair of Dad's boots? I don't want you falling on top of me after all that food you've packed away tonight."

Such sweetness and light! Such cheekiness!

Dressed for outdoors, Elizabeth returned—pockets full of candles and matches—laden with a quilt and lanterns. "Is it okay if I charge my phone awhile in your jalopy? You should plug yours in, too. You'll want to call your folks tomorrow and check on your flight."

He'd forgotten about leaving. He didn't want to think about it.

As they sat in the SUV, Elizabeth asked about William's family and why he was in the States so close to Christmas. She learned his parents died in the family's Cirrus Vision SF50 in a crash in the Peak District and, consequently, William was afraid of flying. She learned sixteen-year-old Georgiana had suffered some trauma but was taking music lessons at a conservatoire and would probably go for a Master of Music. She learned of his Fitzwilliam relatives—"an embarrassing assortment of odd-bods"—and of his friend, Charles—"geek, prankster, tech expert"—who had saved one of the FWD companies from ruin. The havoc had been wreaked by a man named Wickham, a disgruntled former employee with a personal grudge against William.

"And you, Elizabeth? Tell me about yourself. Is there some nice boy-next-door type you're involved with? Some hometown heartthrob?"

He learned, to his relief, there was no man in her life. She was enrolled at an art and design college in nearby Longbourn, taking fashion and textiles, focusing on fibre craft. "So, are you to become a fashion designer? Shall I run into you some day in Milan?"

"Heck, no! I'm a down-home kinda gal. Warm woollen mittens and sweaters are a few of my favourite things, not haute couture. Ugh!"

"So, if not high fashion, what are your aspirations?"

Shrugging, Elizabeth said she'd probably end up teaching like her parents and Jane. William asked why—with such an interest in textiles, a talent for managing, and her skill at turning old, felted sweaters into mitts—she wouldn't make Homespun a real business.

"I told you. It's a fundraiser, not a business."

"Your friend's sister will have the meds she needs. There'll be a donation made to your cause that will cover all expenses."

Elizabeth stammered her thanks, looking down at her hands.

Blimey. I've made her uncomfortable again. Quick, change the subject! "So, tell me about the bizarre over-population of inflatable Santas hereabouts."

He learned Ed owned—amongst other businesses—a discount Christmas store and had offered his profits on that item to Home-spun. The Bennets' neighbours had snapped them all up.

"I like your family, Elizabeth. They're good people, but I could do without Bill's wittering."

She frowned. "You think he's a wit?"

"God, no! I meant he talks long after his audience's interest has gone, assuming there was any interest in the first place. I shan't be subscribing to his YouTube channel or watching his TED Talk... unless I need a cure for insomnia."

Elizabeth yawned. "Speaking of sleep, let's get you settled in the loft."

He fetched his hold-all from the boot, gathered quilt and lanterns, and hung onto Elizabeth for dear life as they trudged through icy snow.

She demonstrated the pull-down staircase and showed him how to add logs to the wood stove. "The light switch is at the top of the—What? Oh, right. No power. Well, that's it, then. Goodnight. I hope you'll sleep well."

Don't go.

"Elizabeth, wait." Flinging aside his armful, William filled the void with her, hugging her tightly and breathing "thank you" into her hair. Quitting the embrace, he reached for her hand, kissing her knuckles.

Elizabeth looked everywhere but at him. Turning back, she told him he was a proper English gentleman after all. "And an old-fashioned one, at that."

"I feel rather old-fashioned tonight. What with no electricity and all…just good company, good food, children, and music." A wistful smile came and went as he gazed around the dim barn. "It's been one of the best Christmas Eves I've spent in a very long time. Maybe ever. Goodnight, Elizabeth, and happy Christmas."

After watching her go, he fed a few logs to the stove, plucked the lantern and duvet from the floor, and climbed the rickety steps to the loft. Shining the light around the tiny space, he spotted a patchwork counterpane on the turned-down bed and what looked like a Quality Street chocolate on the pillow. Twice, before climbing onto the mattress, he banged his head on the slanted walls.

Alone in the dark, in the small—to him—double bed, William listened to the wind howling. Missing Georgiana, he longed to return to the cheery atmosphere next door.

Most of all, he ached for Elizabeth. Unbidden, "All I Want for Christmas" developed into an earworm. *'Cause I just want you here tonight, holding on to me so tight. What more can I do? Baby, all I want for Christmas is you.*

He awoke to total silence, total darkness. *Storm must have passed.* His watch read 3:21. Flinging back the covers, he grabbed a torch. Shivering in only t-shirt and boxers, he plodded to the loo, cursing the cold floor. *Someone said this place would be comfy. Hah! It's as frigid as an ice-box.* Donning casual trousers, Tom Ford checked shirt, and socks from his hold-all, he ran downstairs. *Blast!* The stove was stone cold; the barn had retained no warmth. What had been a cheerful place the day before was all bleakness and lifelessness. *Because she's not here. And she'd know what to do.*

Sitting in the SUV with the heat cranked, William jumped as someone rapped on the driver's side window. At the push of a button, the glass disappeared, revealing the face that had become so precious to him.

"What are you doing?" They spoke at once.

"It's a quarter to four in the morning, and some prat is sitting in his jalopy with the engine running beneath my bedroom window. What are *you* doing out here?"

"I'm afraid I smothered the fire. It's brass monkeys cold over there."

"Why didn't you relight it?"

He looked away, and she suppressed a laugh. "You don't know *how* to start a fire, do you?"

"At home, I simply press a button and—Poof!—the fireplace comes to life."

Elizabeth invited him into the house, saying he could sleep on an air mattress with Noah and Caleb—who was still convinced he was the son of God—or share the futon with Bill. "Just kidding! The boys can climb into bed with their parents for a few hours, and you'll have an air mattress all to yourself. If I wasn't doubled up with little Emily, you could have my bed. I'm wide awake now and won't get back to sleep. It's Christmas morning, after all, and I've got butterflies in my stomach."

"I'm wide awake, too. Join me?"

Fidgeting with the climate control on the passenger side, Elizabeth asked about his family's Christmas traditions.

"Our traditions were just that—traditional. Our home was decorated with holly, ivy, evergreens, and kissing boughs. As children, we wrote to Father Christmas, but, instead of posting the letter, we fed it to the fire so our wish would go up the chimney. We dined on roast goose with all the trimmings, but the pièce de résistance was a flaming plum pudding with a silver charm baked in for good luck in the New Year. At three o'clock, we turned on Auntie Beeb and—"

"Wait. You *what?*"

He laughed at her shocked expression. "We turned on the Beeb—the BBC—for the Royal Christmas broadcast from the Queen. Nowadays, I spend the holidays with the Fitzwilliams, washing down KC caviar on dry toast with Lord Matlock's finest Scotch. He's the 'Uncle Earl' you heard abou—"

His mobile rang, and William switched to hands-free mode. "Hello, Georgie!" To Elizabeth he mouthed, "My sister. Texted her a while ago. It's nine over there."

His caller burst out with "I just have to ask... Did you find the jumper I wanted?"

"Well, happy Christmas to you, too, brat. Explain to me why you need a jumper with *peas* on it. You've always *hated* peas."

"Oh, it's not for me. It's for Anne, who, by the way, woke up with a zit and is now convinced she's dying. I miss you, big brother, and wish you were here. Like, *really*, wish you were here. While everyone slept, Owen and Michael crept down and unwrapped *all* the presents. Aunt Catherine keeps whacking the back of Gerard's knees with her cane. He's been into the Scotch already and is what Richard calls 'legless.' And Rich keeps pestering me to ask about some woman you're crushing on, some Eliz—"

"Whoa, whoa! Just a minute!" Slapping the mobile to his ear, William glanced to his right.

Elizabeth's shoulders were shaking, eyes laughing.

"Sorry, Sis. We were on speakerphone. Yes, she is. Yes, but we're in a parked car, not a— What? No, we're not! Georgiana, stop laughing. Fine! I'm ending this call."

He stabbed the screen and tossed the phone onto the dash. "How do you survive with *four* of them? Sisters," he muttered, drumming fingers on the console.

"They *can* be trying. I was mortified when mine Googled your belongings. But I love them, warts and all, especially at Christmas."

"You're fortunate to be surrounded by people you love and who love you."

"You're making me all teary-eyed." Sniffling, Elizabeth squeezed his hand. "It must be hard to be separated from those *you* love."

I'm not. You're here. William shifted his legs, trying to move closer. A console separated them.

"Wanna move to the backseat?"

"Elizabeth Bennet! Did you just proposition me?"

"Dream on. I asked if *you* wanted to get in the back. I'm fine where *I* am. There's plenty of leg room up here, but you're awfully tall. Back there, you could stretch out."

"If I wanted to stretch out, I'd return to the loft...and freeze. I'd much rather sit here with you and keep warm. Unless..." William waggled his eyebrows. "Wanna join me in the hayloft?"

"Ha, ha. Nice try." Elizabeth unzipped her parka, fished in her pocket for a tissue, and pulled out a spray of greenery. "Huh? Mistletoe? Don't grin at me like that, mister. *I* didn't put it there." He continued his smug stare, and she huffed. "I swear, I didn't!"

Sliding the sprig from between her fingers, William held it above her head. "If we were lovers..." His low, husky voice, little more than a murmur, caught for a moment. "We'd be expected to kiss."

Leaning across the console, he caressed her jaw, turning her face towards his. Short, quick breaths mingled. Lips drew nearer and parted. Eyes closed. Hearts pounded...

And they both jumped out of their skin. Someone was beating on the SUV's fogged-up window. William let loose a barrage of expletives.

"Will!" Bill Collins banged at the glass. "Will! You're not leaving without saying goodbye, are you? I'm sorry about last evening. What? Open the window. I can't hear what you're saying."

"Just as well," William muttered. "Sorry, Elizabeth. I don't normally use such language in mixed company."

"You only said what I was thinking. Now I'm on Santa's naughty list and will find nothing but coal in my stocking. We might as well go in. I need coffee but will settle for tea made on the stove."

The darkest hour was, indeed, just before dawn. William's mood was black, his tea was black, and he was in Bill's black books. *Fine with me. But he'd best not speak a word against Elizabeth or I foresee a black eye in his future. She's a bit of a spitting hellcat when riled.*

The thought made him smile. Everything about her made him smile.

Propping his chin on his hand, he watched Elizabeth flit from cooker to counter to refrigerator—the latter fitted with tubs of icy snow. "What else are you baking there besides baked eggs and mushrooms in toast cups?"

"Blueberry boy bait," she said, peeking in the oven. "Then I'll put the turkey in."

"Boy bait?" He sat back, smirking, stretching out his legs, hooking one arm on the back of the chair.

"Haven't you ever heard the way to a man's heart is through his stomach? If I don't feed you, you'll get—What's the word?—in a strop. Can't have that. The rug rats will be down soon, and you'd scare them away."

The sun rose at 7:11 a.m., as did the entire Bennet household. The lights blinked on, every digital clock flashed 12:00, and William finally got to see Elizabeth's home in all its brightly-lit glory.

By ten, the living room was a colourful shambles of wrapping paper, ribbons, glitter, and bows. Children and pets—sporting bits of sticky tape—romped through a chaos of toys, open boxes, and bubble pack. *A Muppet Family Christmas* played on the telly, and everywhere was laughter, hugging, and squeals of joy—except in the corner where Bill Collins sulked.

"He's just jealous, you know." Elizabeth plunked herself next to William. "For a while I thought he was jealous of you because of me. Truth is, it's quite the opposite. He wanted to be your friend, and I supplanted him. We *are* friends, right?"

Bounding up, she waded through ankle-deep tissue paper and retrieved something from under the tree. She had changed out of her jeans and sweater into a burgundy velvet, wraparound dress, snug in all the right places. His eyes followed her until she handed him a festively-covered box—the kind that might hold a shirt or pyjamas. "Because we're friends, this is for you."

"For me? How did you—? When did you—?" Folding back the

tissue paper, he stared at a soft, shell-pink jumper with an embroidered "Peas on Earth" appliqué. It wasn't an exact match to the photo on his mobile, but the differences were subtle.

"Do you suppose it will fit?" Elizabeth bit on a cuticle, raising anxious eyes to his.

Holding the fluffy creation against his chest, he sadly shook his head.

"Ow!" Rubbing his arm, he told her she packed quite a punch for such a slight person. "It's lovely, Elizabeth. Thank you. I'm sure Georgie and Anne will thank you. And I must thank Mrs. whatshername for relinquishing it."

"She didn't." Bending her head, picking at the troublesome cuticle, Elizabeth told him she had finished stitching it at three thirty that very morning. "It's the sweater from the barn...the one you plucked from the clothesline and push—"

In his authoritative, F. William Darcy tone, he addressed the room. "Excuse us a moment."

Standing and taking Elizabeth's hand, he whispered, "Come with me?" At her nod, he led her to the front hall.

Still holding her hand, he took a deep breath. "When I remember what I said yesterday and how I behaved around you, your sisters, and your neighbours, I am deeply, deeply ashamed. I don't deserve that gift, Elizabeth, but I thank you for it. And I thank you for being the warmhearted, beautiful person I've come to admire and respect and..." He gulped.

His words became more rushed. "I know it's too soon. We haven't known one another for even a full day. But I feel as though I've known you forever. I've been searching for you that long. But if you don't feel the same, just tell me now. If it's what you want, I'll walk away and—"

"Don't!"

Don't? Don't what? Don't keep talking? Don't walk away?

Elizabeth sniffled. "Don't walk away. *Please.*"

Pulling her into his arms, he stroked Elizabeth's hair, whispering, "I'm not walking away. I'm not going *anywhere.*"

"Yes, you are. You're going home, to England." Her sniffles turned into sobs.

"In a while…for a while, yes. But I not only have a watch with dual time-zones, I have dual citizenship. And a flat in New York. We'll make it work, Elizabeth, I promise."

Digging in the pocket of his Zilli coat, he found the crushed sprig of greenery. *Pathetic but still functional, I hope.*

Holding the mistletoe above their heads, he spoke in a low husky voice. "If we were lovers, we'd be expected to kiss."

Caressing her jaw, his lips drew nearer to hers and parted. Short, quick breaths mingled. Eyes closed. Hearts pounded as William and Elizabeth shared the snog of a lifetime.

Two women spied on them from the living room door while "Feliz Navidad" played in the background.

"They certainly seem to be having a good time out there." Martha Gardiner smirked.

Her sister-in-law nodded. "I love seeing young people so happy. Do you suppose that's the same sprig of mistletoe I slipped into Liz's pocket?"

PART 3: IT'S GOING TO BE A WONDERFUL LIFE

Free from tension and anxiety but impatient to arrive, William decelerated, and his red Range Rover SVAutobiography Dynamic exited I-95 North.

His week had been nothing short of a whirlwind. *Rearranging appointments, cancelling meetings, breaking the news to the Fitzwilliam oddbods, visiting the jeweller to approve the bespoke engagement ring.*

The temperature rose above zero. Flurries turned to intermittent showers and fallen snow to slush as the sign welcoming him to "Merryton" came into view. *Welcome sight, indeed!*

Just under a year ago, he had driven the same winding road, surrounded by bucolic scenery. But nothing—*Nothing!*—was so beautiful to him as the sight of Elizabeth and her family waving to him from the front porch of the farmhouse.

Laughing as she slipped and slid her way to the driveway, Elizabeth hardly waited for the SUV to come to a complete stop before opening his door and flinging herself at him. But with her whole family watching, their reunion was more circumspect than he preferred. *There's always the hayloft, later.*

"Are you wearing it?"

Rolling his eyes as they stepped through the slush, William unbuttoned his Zilli coat, revealing a reindeer jumper with a "You Sleigh Me" appliqué. "And you?"

Unzipping her eggplant parka—"Ta-da!"—Elizabeth showed off her sweater's embroidered patch which sported a reindeer with long lashes and red lipstick and the words "Olive the Other Reindeer."

"God, woman!" William wrapped an arm around Elizabeth's waist as she lost her footing. "Careful of the icy patch! Why aren't you wearing your boots?"

"I was in such a hurry to greet you, it must have slipped my mind. I hope, though, that *someone* will catch me if I fall."

"It's a bit of a role reversal for us, but turnabout *is* fair play." Scooping her up into his arms and pointing out his new Timberland boots, William said, "I've already fallen for *you*...over and over and over again."

J. MARIE CROFT is a self-proclaimed word nerd and adherent of Jane Austen's quote "Let other pens dwell on guilt and misery." Bearing witness to Joanne's fondness for *Pride and Prejudice*, wordplay, and laughter are her light-hearted novel, *Love at First Slight* (a Babblings of a Bookworm Favourite Read of 2014), her playful novella, *A Little Whimsical in His Civilities* (Just Jane 1813's Favourite 2016 JAFF Novella), and her humorous short stories in the anthologies *Sun-kissed*, *The Darcy Monologues*, *Dangerous to Know*, and *Rational Creatures*. Unlike William and Elizabeth, Joanne lives in Nova Scotia, Canada.

THE SEASON FOR FRIENDLY MEETINGS

ANNGELA SCHROEDER

At Christmas every body invites their friends and thinks little of even the worst weather. —Jane Austen

With the promise of her daughters being amongst eligible rich men, Mrs. Bennet had wasted no time in giving consent for them to accompany Mrs. Long and her nieces to Yorkshire for the Christmas holidays. Elizabeth Bennet was not one to discount her good fortune. Any opportunity to engage in society was something she relished, but even more as her favorite sister still nursed a broken heart.

Had Mr. Bingley returned to Netherfield Hall after his London business was concluded, the tenuous circumstances in which we find ourselves would be immaterial.

But he had not, and therefore, with no understanding between Jane and Mr. Bingley and Elizabeth rejecting a marriage proposal from her horrible cousin Mr. Collins, Mrs. Bennet was ready to exile her second daughter anywhere.

With a peck on the cheek, her mother said, "I sincerely hope your Christmas may abound in the gaieties which the season generally brings, dear Jane. I daresay you will return to us engaged, if Mrs. Long has anything to do with it. And Lizzy, do not run on in a wild manner. Mind where you are."

The Long nieces had diverted Elizabeth and Jane Bennet every summer for as far back as the girls could remember. With their departure to the North before the single and wealthy Mr. Bingley departed Netherfield for London, they were only aware of Jane's disappointment by letters from their aunt.

Elizabeth looked about the ballroom in wonder. Swags of crimson fabric draped the columns with boughs of pine hanging from mantles and bannisters. Candles illuminated the mirrors set to reflect the light throughout the rooms. *Mama would delight in the attention paid to the decorations.*

Her light heart froze at the sight of Jane, who was dancing with a smartly turned out officer in Regimentals. Hoping to see a bloom in her sister's cheeks, she saw none. Instead, her sister's countenance still showed signs of anguish. *But only to me. I know her almost as well as she knows herself.*

At that moment, the set ended, and the officer escorted Jane toward Elizabeth.

"Colonel Fitzwilliam, may I introduce you to my sister, Miss Elizabeth Bennet? Lizzy, this is Colonel Fitzwilliam of Matlock House."

After making a fine leg, the colonel said, "Miss Elizabeth, your sister tells me you are staying at Dronfield with the Miss Longs."

"Yes. Miss Agatha Long and Miss Helen are dear friends, and their cousins the Thorns were so kind to invite us for Christmastide."

"Berty Thorn and Miss Clarissa Thorn are the best of people. And you will find no ball as merry as the Somerset's Christmas ball." The girls nodded, and he continued. "I understand you are from the South? Hertfordshire?"

"We are, sir. Are you familiar with the area?"

"No. I believe my father has spoken of it from visiting as a youth, and my cousin was most recently in the area at a friend's estate, but I have no connection."

"That is unfortunate, Colonel, as it is the most beautiful land in the country."

"But are you not biased, Miss Elizabeth?" he asked with a crooked grin.

Delighted, she laughed. "I confess I am, sir. My intent is to convince all of the superiority of our little hamlet."

Pleasantries were exchanged, and the colonel offered to fetch the ladies some refreshments. Soon after, Agatha and Helen came scampering up to the Bennets.

"Jane, Lizzy, you will never guess what we *just* heard."

"I am certain we cannot."

Agatha looked over her shoulder and turned back before lowering her voice barely above a whisper. "It is only that—"

"Speak up," Helen said, nudging her side.

"I can only speak so loudly," she hissed.

Agatha signaled for the girls to follow her to a small alcove.

"What we have to divulge is not polite for ballroom conversation, so it would be best to guard our privacy."

"Then maybe we should not be discussing it at all," interjected Jane.

Agatha dismissed Jane's admonishment without a thought and continued on. "I have just had it from my cousin Albert's dear friend that Mr. Wickham is a man not to be trusted."

Elizabeth recoiled in shock. "How came you to speak of Mr. Wickham this far removed from Meryton? That is most unusual *and* unexpected, Aggie." The childhood nickname rolled off her tongue as she felt her ire rising.

"I mentioned I was from Meryton, and Lord Somerset said he understood a scamp he once knew from Derbyshire joined the local militia and now resided in that village. That his name was Wickham, and I would do best to stay away from him."

Elizabeth felt her jaw tighten. "I am tired of the rich mercilessly trouncing the character of a man who was thrown into circumstances beneath his due."

"Lizzy! Lower your voice," Jane pleaded, glancing about the room.

Elizabeth realized her error and leaned in. "Of what did your cousin's friend accuse him? The same crime as others before? That his father was a steward?" She raised her chin and waited for a reply.

Helen looked about, furrowing her brows. "No, Lizzy," she said in a whisper, "his crimes were much greater than that." She swallowed, and her sister nodded, encouraging the elder Miss Long to continue. "It seems he has attempted to…to ruin a young woman."

"In all truth, more than one," Agatha cut in.

Elizabeth inhaled a slow breath to calm her agitation. "And how do you know this? Who has brought this claim?"

"Why, Lord Somerset's valet told him. He said his batman informed him after hearing it from the maids in the kitchen."

"The maids in the kitchen?"

"Lizzy, again, you *must* lower your voice," Jane said.

Lizzy turned sharply before replying. "Jane, do you know how a man's character could be permanently maligned by listening to idle gossip in a ballroom? Or, as in this case, even the kitchens? With much pain, Mr. Wickham told me the wrongs committed against him by Mr. Darcy. How his future was ripped away by *that man* solely due to jealousy. I am sorry, Helen, Aggie"—turning to her friends—"you have no ally in me. I cannot give merit to claims against a man I know in my heart is good."

The girls looked from Elizabeth to each other.

"Lizzy," Jane began, "might we have given too much credence to Mr. Wickham's words? We only know what he has told us."

"My dear Jane. You are so tender-hearted that you do not want to believe ill of Mr. Darcy. However, Mr. Wickham has such a countenance of goodness about him, I would assure you of his truthfulness.

"Now," she continued, looking up and seeing Colonel Fitzwilliam approaching them with two glasses of negus. "Let us push these thoughts from our mind and enjoy the holiday. We are at a Christmas ball, after all."

Elizabeth turned to smile, hiding her irritation and extending her hand to the proffered glass. "Thank you, Colonel."

Agatha and Helen curtseyed and excused themselves to find their partners for the next set, each glancing at Elizabeth and then Jane.

I cannot believe they would spread falsehoods. The poor man cannot escape his mistreatment no matter what part of the country he is in.

Lizzy looked up and blushed at Colonel Fitzwilliam's expectant eyes. "My apologies, Colonel. I was not attending."

"If you are otherwise unengaged, might I have the pleasure of the next dance?" he asked as the musicians began to tune their instruments.

"I would be pleased to continue our earlier conversation about my fair Hertfordshire."

She smiled at Jane as she set her glass on a table, taking the colonel's hand. They joined the set as the music commenced.

"Is this your first trip to Yorkshire?" he asked, circling her.

"Yes, and we are quite enchanted with the moors. It is beautiful country." She then circled him.

"But it still pales in comparison to your own part of the world?" A grin spread at the corners of his mouth as he took her hand.

"Of course."

"Miss Elizabeth, might I ask if something was said to disturb you?" They were separated by the dance for a moment until he returned to face her. "You appear distracted."

Am I so obvious? She smiled as they progressed down the set. "I am merely a young woman from a small estate far removed from society. I am unaccustomed to the...heated attacks some might place upon others. I have...a dislike for those who would malign the character of a worthy man who does not deserve it."

He nodded. "That is commendable. No matter ones' origins, proper behavior should be celebrated. I cannot condone speaking ill of one solely due to their lack of wealth, circumstances, or rumors."

"I believe you are in the minority of the *ton,* sir. Others I have met seem to take great joy in just that—decrying a man's character solely for being...socially beneath them."

He moved around her again as they clasped hands. "Miss Elizabeth. Although I am the son of an earl, I am the *second* born. I have had to make my way through His Majesty's Army, my life having been saved by those whom society deems *beneath* me. I do not share the same view as my peers, for I know the true value of a man is in his character and not his title or land."

A radiant smile spread across her countenance.

"I also know that many men's lives have been ruined through speculation and idle gossip in a ballroom and at card parties, and I have no patience for that."

She drew a deep breath, feeling gratitude. "Colonel, your words give me hope that not all men are as unfeeling as those I have recently come in contact with."

"Now, I cannot promise you that," he said, laughing as he separated from her. "But I do not hold the only bit of merit in the room. Why my cousin, for example—the one I told you about who visited your home county—he is a much better man than myself. He actually should be here, but I have yet to see him." He looked toward the door and around the room before his eyes settled back on her. "Might I ask what brought this line of thought about?"

It must be the punch. How odd this conversation. With a stranger. She separated from him in the dance, before returning to take his hand again. "A gentleman Miss Long was dancing with claims to have knowledge of a friend. Although he is a recent acquaintance, I am disturbed by the pains that have been taken to ruin this man's prospects."

The colonel raised an eyebrow. "Forgive me for saying so, but I have taken the measure of your character. You do not appear to me as other women who practice histrionics. These are heavy claims indeed."

"Indeed, Colonel. This young man has shown great courage when his life should have proceeded in an entirely different direction. He has had to make his own way because the path chosen by his godfather was stolen from him."

The colonel stiffened. He used the movements of the dance to consider his next words, then asked, "And this man? What of his story? Might I be of assistance?"

"He was the son of a steward on an estate but a day's ride from Yorkshire. He was loved by all, most notably his godfather, the owner of the estate. At his own father's death, his godfather took him in and educated him, promising him a living of the church when it came available. He has told me it was his fondest wish, and I do believe he would have made a fine clergyman. He was educated alongside the heir to the estate, and therein lies the problem."

"A problem? A gentleman's education granted by the estate owner sounds very generous. Surely, this young man must have used the schooling provided for him to secure his future. Is he a rector near your father's estate?"

"No...no, he is not," she said, stopping mid-step and almost causing the other dancers to collide with her. The colonel moved her along, keeping their place in line.

He quirked a brow, and his low voice sounded strained. "Do you mean, he has *not* taken up a position in the field that he studied for? A clergyman is an honorable vocation, and a man of the caliber you are speaking most assuredly would fit that field."

"Yes...yes he would, but he is in the militia."

"The militia? Well, then I am certain he offers spiritual guidance to those in his company. A man of that ilk, one whose 'fondest wish' is to serve the Lord, would have a moral example emanating from him at all times, do you not agree?"

"Yes..."

"I am sure in your interactions with him he has proven himself a most worthy gentleman–no mockery of others, kindness to all, proper behavior in the company of ladies, guarded speeches..."

"Yes..."

"Now, what was mentioned about the heir? He who your friend was raised with?"

Elizabeth swallowed, her feelings on the subject of Mr. Wickham beginning to cloud with uncertainty. "You have given my mind much to think on, sir, but of the heir, I have no question. I have met him myself, and a more selfish, taciturn, proud, and arrogant man I have never encountered."

The colonel smiled. "And what is the impetus for these accusations?"

"He denied my friend his promised legacy upon the death of his father."

"I am all astonishment. Was there no legal redress?"

Elizabeth cocked her head. "No...no there was not. My friend said it was a gentleman's agreement between his godfather and himself."

Colonel Fitzwilliam nodded. "Then I am certain the heir to the estate received his due, censored by his own people, when it was discovered he did not follow through with his father's wishes."

She grew quiet again, his words heavy on her mind. "No, sir. My friend said he could not wound the son without wounding the memory of the father. He has told no one else."

"No one else?"

"I will concede...it appears he may have...told of his sorrows to a few other people in the village."

The colonel clasped hands with the woman on his left to promenade before returning to his position across from Elizabeth. "And what of this heir? You say you have met him and were able to discern his character after the conversation you had with your friend?"

"No. That only confirmed my opinions of him. When I first met him, we were in a ballroom, and ladies outnumbered gentlemen. More than one was without a partner, and he refused to dance."

"That is a crime indeed," he replied, winking before handing her to another member of their group. Upon her return, he said, "And with such manners, I am certain his deceitful character was evident?"

She shook her head. "No...no, I do not believe he is deceitful. In truth, I would call him...painfully candid." She sniffed. "But, that does not excuse his conduct toward my friend!"

"No, it does not. The unfortunate clergyman who is now a member of the militia? It is unlucky he has yet to procure a respectable position in a parish. Do you believe this villain, this heir, is to blame for that as well?"

She was quiet as the dance separated them, and her thoughts rambled with new concerns. *Why "is" Mr. Wickham not a clergyman if he was trained up as such? His manners are engaging and friendly. He should have made many connections at school which would precipitate another position amongst other estate owners.* "Colonel, do *you* believe he has been singled out by this heir? That other estate owners will not appoint him in the position because of their allegiance to that man's wealth?"

"Miss Elizabeth. In my experience, a man of worth will be recognized by those of equal worth. If this man is truly as decent as he presents himself to be, others will see it. Do you think it is possible he has misrepresented his own character?"

As the set ended, he said, "Forgive me. It is evident by your countenance I have troubled you. Are you displeased with me?"

"No, sir. You *have* given me much to consider."

"Might I ask when your friend told you his tale?"

Elizabeth gasped, the realization of her words slowly coming forth. "At a card party."

"At a card party? How remarkable. *We* do not wish to ruin *this* man's reputation by speaking *his* name in a public setting, yet..."

He let the thought linger, and Elizabeth felt her cheeks burn.

"Miss Bennet, are you unwell? You are quite flushed."

"I believe I need to rest. Forgive me?"

"Of course. Let us leave the ballroom, and I will have someone find your sister." He steadied her arm, and as they continued through the room, he slowed at Lord Somerset's side. "Cyril, could you please see that Miss Jane Bennet is brought to the library? And might you find my cousin? Send him as well."

FITZWILLIAM DARCY HATED BALLS. It was not the dancing he despised, (he actually quite enjoyed that pastime). It was the simpering misses and their calculating mothers; it was the crush of people and the speculation of who he would dance with; it was not being at home with a good book but instead on display as a fishmonger's goods. Because of that, he had learned years before that the only way to keep the gossip at bay was to limit his dancing to those in his own party.

A pair of brown eyes flashed through his mind. A delicate upturned nose and rosy bow-shaped lips.

And *that* was why they found themselves at a Christmas ball in snowy weather miles from his great-uncle's estate! He had not wanted to come tonight but believed a diversion was necessary—away from another quiet evening filled with remembrances of the Bennet sisters of Longbourn.

Her smile. Her laugh. Her impertinent remarks haunted him. It had been a month since they departed Hertfordshire, and he still felt her loss.

He handed his coat to the footman, grateful for his old friend Cyril's invitation. The ballroom was festively dressed with boughs of holly, and the wax candles lit the space with a merry glow. He greeted Lady Somerset and made his rounds, shaking hands and accepting the wishes of the holiday.

"Darcy, you have arrived!" a jolly Lord Somerset said, his hand extended.

"Yes, Cyril. The road from Hollowridge was not altogether clear, but my drivers managed, as they always do."

"I am surprised the weather dared to defy you, Fitzwilliam Darcy. The last storm to do so buried three feet of snow over our tree fort overnight, remember?"

Darcy grinned at the memory. "How could I forget? We both prayed for no snow but then had our ears boxed for sneaking out of the schoolroom to have a snowball fight."

"Yes. And Richard had it worst of all!"

Bingley interrupted. "I know the colonel can be impulsive and mischievous, but of what do you accuse him?"

"Accuse him, nothing!" Cyril replied. "He *assailed* Nanny with snowballs when she found us outside."

"And therefore, he could not hear for two days, nor could he sit for three!" Darcy shook his head. "Most of my childhood adventures involved Richard and the mighty scrapes in which we found ourselves. That still holds true today, even though we are men and have left the schoolroom far behind."

"That is right. Which reminds me...Richard asked me to send you to the library when I saw you."

"The library? That does not sound like his regular haunt at a ball."

Cyril waggled his eyebrows before replying. "He had two very lovely ladies with him and asked for you to join them. If I did not know him better, I would accuse Richard of preparing for another "adventure." However, I do. Knowing he is *not* like his brother, the viscount, the young ladies' reputations are likely intact. Although," he said, pointing in the direction of the library, "Richard may be a gentleman, I have no idea if the ladies are mercenary."

Darcy felt himself tense at his host's jest. He thanked Cyril and turned in the direction of the library, his feet thundering down the corridor.

At least the door is open, and a footman is without.

As he approached the library door, he heard his cousin say, "My only wish is to help those who cannot help themselves," but he stopped altogether when he heard another voice answer:

"I do not know what to say, Colonel. I am uncertain of whom to believe."

Elizabeth! His heart raced, and he felt his breathing increase. *She is here? Elizabeth is here? Is fate toying with me?* He was about to interrupt when—

"Mr. Wickham... But, Mr. Wickham assured me through his manners and countenance that he was of the utmost character, and another gentleman, whom I shall not name, is not. I worry that I believed him solely due to my own vanity."

Richard, who was seated facing Miss Elizabeth and her sister Jane Bennet, saw him in the doorway and, at once, stayed him with a glance.

"I have only known Mr.—pardon me—the man to be unfeeling and arrogant. I am attempting to reconsider my dealings with him and am confused at best. But, as my dear Jane has said before, maybe we misjudged him."

"There must be no blame, Miss Elizabeth," he said, raising a brow in Darcy's direction. "*George Wickham* has used people ill his whole life. You are not the first kind-hearted woman who has been deceived by his charms."

He heard her gasp. "You have known his name all along?"

Richard nodded. "The story you related sounded too familiar. We, my cousin and I have dealt with Wickham's proclivities for many years. We have settled his affairs and...things which are not for the sensibilities of ladies... I am only grateful he did not take advantage of more than your trust."

Her head shook and the curls at the back of her neck bounced against her porcelain skin. Darcy cursed himself for letting her be so ill-informed, unprotected.

I should never have encouraged Bingley to leave Hertfordshire. Had we stayed, I would have declared myself, and shielded her from Wickham... Yes, I would have! Hang my family's expectations! I will be with the woman I love!

Richard's voice broke through his thoughts, and he was about to interrupt when the question caught him. "And what of this man, the heir to the estate where Wickham grew up? Are your feelings toward him altered in the slightest?"

"I cannot say," he heard her say.

Bingley let out an almost audible gasp as he *finally* realized with whom Richard was conversing. Darcy indicated to remain silent but believed he would have to restrain the man when *his angel* began to speak.

"Lizzy, I am no better than you. You must not be too hard on yourself. It is not I whom Mr. D–whom the gentleman insulted at the Meryton assembly. Your pride was injured."

"He *insulted* you, Miss Elizabeth? In a public assembly?" Richard stifled a snort. "The devil he did! And what did he say?"

The room was silent as Darcy stepped forward. "I misspoke."

Jane and Elizabeth both stood and whipped around to face him. "I misspoke," he repeated softly, "and can only pray the lady find it in her heart to forgive my falsehood."

She is mute, and Miss Bennet is terrified, fool!

"It is obvious that I now have other wrongs to atone for, ladies, and both Bingley and I beg your forgiveness."

Elizabeth colored when her eyes met his; Jane Bennet blanched upon seeing Bingley.

"Oh, Darce. You are in a fine fettle, are you not? Now, come and let us unravel this tangled ball of yarn you have created. Sit there, beside Miss Elizabeth. And you, Bingley, there, by Miss Bennet."

Awkward bowing, curtsies, and even more uncomfortable greetings supervened before everyone took their seats.

"Miss Bennet, what a happy surprise this is. I trust your family is well and preparing for the holidays?" Bingley asked, a cautious crack in his voice.

"Yes, th-thank you, sir," Jane said, keeping her gaze lowered.

Richard laughed again before continuing on his cause. "Now, Miss Elizabeth. You appear to be a woman who is not afraid to voice her thoughts, no matter what they may be. I believe now is an opportunity for you to ask my cousin himself."

Darcy cringed at the gasp which came from Elizabeth's lips, while Richard chuckled. "Oh, I was remiss to mention that fact. At any rate, I am certain my cousin Fitzwilliam would be delighted to answer for any sins you believe he may have committed or other accusations laid before him. After all, we do not want a man's reputation maligned in a ballroom or even in a *library*, for that matter, do we, Miss Elizabeth? We are aware of the great disservice such occurrences would have for an honorable man."

"Yes," he heard her say softly.

He held his breath as her eyes cautiously rose to meet his.

ELIZABETH BENNET HAD ONLY ONCE BEFORE FELT so mistaken. She had the same strange sensation of when she was a girl of eight and how she was still learning a valuable lesson from that day. She had accused a servant of taking her beloved copy of Spencer's "The Faerie Queene." The book had been in the sitting room the day before when the new maid came in to clean, but later it was gone.

Elizabeth worked the fabric of her skirt between her fingers, the shame of both events coloring her features. Her papa had asked the girl, she had denied any knowledge of the book, and he had terminated her without a thought. Young Lizzy was all righteous indignation until she had discovered the book had slipped between the slats of her bed.

She had run down the stairs to her father's study and begged him to hire the girl back, but he refused. "What kind of master would I be, Lizzy, if I changed my mind so quickly?" he had asked. "No, I will have Mrs. Hill send her to your uncle Phillips. Your aunt needs a new parlor maid, and this girl will do."

As she began to walk from the room, he had called to her with words she thought she had taken to heart. "My Lizzy," he had said.

"Let this be a lesson to you. You must never judge the character of others without first looking at your own faults. You often fall asleep reading, and this is not the first time a book has slipped through your bed slats. Someday, it could be much worse..."

AND NOW, *here I am, thirteen years later, and still judging too quickly.*

She took a deep breath before she began. "You must forgive me. As has happened in the past, I have a tendency to speak too openly when a perceived injustice has been committed. My apologies to all whom I have offended."

"There has been no offense–"

"But, you, Colonel," she said turning quickly, "you have played a mean trick, keeping us at a disadvantage."

The colonel pressed his hand to his heart and grinned. "Do forgive me, Miss Elizabeth. You must see I had no choice. If I had told you of my connection to Darcy, you would have discounted my testimony, believing it to be only out of loyalty to my cousin, so I could not. That alone kept me silent while I attempted to guide you to your own conclusions."

Elizabeth heard the words of the colonel but could not fully attend them. How could she when *he* was there?

He, whom she was immediately drawn to at the Meryton assembly but who had deemed her only tolerable. *He,* whom she could not rid from her thoughts, even when she attempted to mask her feelings of attraction with the hatred Mr. Wickham subscribed to. *He,* whose conversations she debated and challenged so she could remain in control of her faculties as his equal and not dissolve into a simpering, silly miss as other women had.

She felt *his* eyes on her like fingers on her skin, causing a flush of heat to climb her throat. "If what you say is true, Colonel, then I owe my deepest apologies to"—she looked up and met his gaze—"to you, Mr. Darcy."

Their eyes held until, flustered, she looked away. In an instant, he stood and extended his hand. She instinctively reached for it.

"It is I who must apologize to you. You have been nothing but who you are—an honest and loyal friend, seeking out the good in those who deserve it. Had my pride not limited my willingness to expose him for what he truly was, you, an intelligent woman, would not have been deceived."

He cleared his throat. "Richard, would you do me the honor of introducing me to your acquaintance?" he asked, never taking his eyes from her.

A smirk spread across the colonel's lips. "Miss Elizabeth Bennet, may I present my cousin, Mr. Fitzwilliam Darcy of Pemberley, Derbyshire."

She nodded her head.

"It is a pleasure to meet you, madam."

"And you as well, sir."

He bowed and kissed her gloved hand. "Might I request the next dance, as well as the supper set?"

She furrowed her brow. "Two dances? Mr. Darcy, whatever will people say?" Shocked to see a tug at the corner of his lips and a deep dimple in his left cheek, Lizzy's composure faltered.

"I believe, madam," he said, his deep, rich baritone enveloping her, "that this is the season for friendly meetings. I find that nothing would give me more pleasure than standing up with the handsomest woman of my acquaintance." He slowly rubbed his thumb across her knuckles. "If you will accept?"

The room was silent, save his breathing and the crackle of the fire behind him. Her eyes sparkled as an unexpected new sensation raced through her.

She bit her lip and glanced up at him through thick lashes. "Well, as you say, sir. It is Christmas."

ANNGELA SCHROEDER HAS a degree in English with a concentration in British literature and a master's in education. She has taught high school for twenty years and could imagine no job as fulfilling (other than maybe being Oprah). She loves to travel, bake, and watch college football with her husband of eighteen years and three rambunctious sons. Her weaknesses are yellow cake with chocolate frosting, her father's Arabic food (namely grape leaves and falafel), and frozen Girl Scout Thin Mints. She lives in California where she dreams of Disney adventures and trips across the pond. Follow her on Twitter: @schros2000, Instagram: Anngela Schroeder-Author, and Facebook.

MISTLETOE MISMANAGEMENT

ELIZABETH ADAMS

A scheme of which every part promises delight, can never be successful; and general disappointment is only warded off by the defense of some little peculiar vexation. —Jane Austen

*M*ust you hang that?"

Elizabeth looked over her shoulder and smiled at her husband of nearly a month. "It's tradition!" She carefully arranged holly in the kissing bough, then reached for a sprig of mistletoe. "I would have thought you would appreciate the opportunity to steal a kiss in the drawing room."

He wrapped his arms around her from behind and pulled her close to him, pressing his nose into her neck. "I enjoy stealing kisses in every room, but I would appreciate not having an audience." He planted a kiss on her neck and pinched her side in the spot he knew she was most ticklish.

She squealed and leapt away. "Mr. Darcy!"

He easily pulled her back to him and leaned close to her ear. "I should not like other gentlemen trying to steal a kiss from my wife, either."

She flushed. "I shouldn't like that either. Would you feel more at ease if I were to promise not to stand under the bough unless you are with me?"

"I would. And be careful when you are walking with Fitzwilliam. He is likely to lead you directly to it."

Elizabeth laughed. "He would not! He thinks of me as another sister."

Darcy raised a brow and looked at her silently for a moment. "As you say, dearest."

ELIZABETH STOOD in the entryway of Pemberley prepared to greet Darcy's family. They had been introduced when they were betrothed; his aunt and uncle, Lord and Lady Aldrington, had kindly hosted a dinner for them in London. However, Elizabeth suspected it was more for the sake of appearances and maintaining the connection to their nephew and niece than for true support of her or their marriage. She decided that it did not matter why they were being kind to her so long as they were kind. And slight though it may be, they were supporting her husband in their own way.

Colonel Fitzwilliam had supported their marriage in truth. He had spoken well of Elizabeth to his parents and brothers, and he had already placed a bet in the books at White's guessing at the date of their first child's birth. Elizabeth blushed to the roots of her hair when she heard how early the most popular bets were. Nevertheless, he had been their staunchest ally and she was nothing but appreciative. Her dear husband had given up much to wed her—she realized that now—and she would do everything in her power to safeguard his family relationships.

She knew he was not sorry to lose his aunt, Lady Catherine de Burgh, though Elizabeth felt the weight of the break and hoped to eventually heal the breach in the family. But she understood it was a matter of pride for Fitzwilliam, the best sort of pride, to not admit his aunt to their homes until she apologized to his wife and reined in her behavior. Elizabeth would not push him, but she felt the pressure of this visit all the more because of it.

Darcy and Miss Darcy—or Georgiana, as Elizabeth had recently begun calling her—had traditionally spent the festive season with his mother's family. Their father had only had one sibling—a sister who married a man with a large estate in Cornwall. She had seldom visited Pemberley after her marriage, and she had died more than ten years before. Darcy and Georgiana were not close with their cousins, more due to distance than inclination; in contrast, the Fitzwilliam family lived in Staffordshire only fifty miles away.

The last several years had been spent at their uncle's estate. This year, his aunt had suggested they come to Pemberley now that it had a mistress.

Elizabeth saw the suggestion for what it was: an opportunity to test her mettle. She refused to be intimidated and went about preparing for the holiday and their visit as she would have regardless of their guests. Rooms were appointed and aired out, gifts were purchased and wrapped, meals were chosen, and gowns were retrimmed. The baskets were ordered for Boxing Day, and everything was prepared.

She ordered greenery to be collected and set about making garlands for the house. Elizabeth then asked Mrs. Reynolds which housemaids and footmen had the most artistic ability, followed by an afternoon showing those chosen how she wished the garlands strung together and hung. Mrs. Reynolds found a few crates of decorations in the attics, and Elizabeth and Georgiana spent several afternoons happily gilding the house with ribbons and baubles. When they finished their decorating, they practiced carols in the music room— Georgiana on the pianoforte and Elizabeth singing, much to the appreciation of Mr. Darcy.

Now Elizabeth had done all she could to prepare, and the family had been seen arriving at the gate. Darcy helped her with her cloak, and she stepped out on his arm to greet the approaching carriage.

She would not be intimidated. She would not. Everything was in place and she was fully prepared for any eventuality. Her courage would rise—it always did.

SHORTLY AFTER HIS FAMILY ARRIVED, Darcy hurried everyone into the house and out of the cold. Colonel Fitzwilliam wasted no time kissing Elizabeth on her rosy cheek, then winking at her husband when he caught his eye. Darcy looked heavenward and led his aunt to the stairs.

"Your rooms are prepared, and tea will be ready in the blue drawing room in an hour's time," Elizabeth said to the weary travelers.

"Thank you, my dear," said Lord Aldrington. "We shall see you in an hour." He led his lady up the stairs when it looked as if she might say something contradictory.

His eldest son and daughter-in-law, Lord and Lady Lisle, followed behind, looking cold and tired and, in the lady's case, more than a little cross. Elizabeth hoped a rest would set her to rights.

Colonel Fitzwilliam stayed behind a moment talking to Georgiana. "Am I in my usual room, Elizabeth?"

Darcy bristled at hearing his wife's name on his cousin's silver tongue.

"Actually, no. Fitzwilliam thought you would be more comfortable in the guest wing."

The colonel raised his brows and looked at his cousin. Darcy stared steadfastly over Fitzwilliam's shoulder.

"Martin will show you the way." She gestured to a footman waiting near the stairs.

"I hope you haven't put me too close to Lisle," he groused. "He snores something awful and you know he walks about in his sleep. I'm liable to wake up with him standing above me or worse!"

"Do stop moaning, Fitz," Darcy said impatiently. "Come, I will take you up myself." He dismissed the footman and pulled his cousin toward the stairs, leaving his wife and sister trying to hide their smiles.

"What was that all about, Fitz?" asked the colonel when they reached the top of the stairs.

"You know very well, and don't call me Fitz, Fitz!"

"You started it," grumbled the colonel. "Now tell me, Darcy"—he emphasized his cousin's name—"why you unceremoniously dragged me away from your lovely wife and sister."

"I did not unceremoniously drag you. As per usual, you have a gift for hyperbole. And you know very well why you were removed from the ladies. You flirt too much for your own good, Fitzwilliam, and one day, you'll flirt with the wrong lady and that will be the end of it for you." Darcy opened the door to his cousin's room and preceded him inside.

The colonel shut the door behind them and rounded on Darcy. "Are you suggesting that I have done so today? Or that I was flirting with my cousin's wife? Or my own ward?" asked the colonel, a horrified expression on his face when he mentioned Georgiana.

"No, of course you were not flirting with Georgie, you never do." The colonel relaxed slightly. "But you *were* flirting with Mrs. Darcy."

Fitzwilliam straightened again. "I was not. I have a very friendly relationship with Elizabeth, as a friend and as a cousin."

"Even when you speak of her you sound as if you are flirting!"

The colonel spluttered. "How is that even possible!"

"Believe me, if it were possible to flirt with a woman who is not present, you would be the man to achieve it."

The colonel shook his head. "I do not know how Elizabeth puts up with your addlepated head. I'm surprised she hasn't thrown a book at you yet."

"That's another thing. You should not call her Elizabeth."

"She asked me to!"

"She *what?*" cried Darcy.

"At the wedding breakfast. She said we were cousins now and, as you and I are so close, I should call her Elizabeth. I was rather proud to be asked, if I may say so. She didn't make the offer to anyone else."

"Your family was not at the wedding," Darcy bit out.

"You know what I mean." The colonel paced a few steps away and turned back to his cousin. "I asked her to call me Richard. It seemed the gentlemanly thing to do."

Darcy felt heat rush to his face. "Has she taken you up on your offer?"

"I do not recall. She may have, once, at the wedding. If she did, it was done in a public setting and entirely out of familial feeling. Surely you do not doubt her, man!"

"No! Of course not!" Now Darcy looked horrified. "But I do not like to hear you saying her name, and I do not wish to hear her saying yours."

The colonel tilted his head and smiled at his cousin. "Darcy, you have nothing to worry about, from me or any other man. I would never do that to you, as you well know, and even if I were half the rogue you think me, Elizabeth would never consider dishonoring you in such a way. Firstly, because she is too good, and secondly, because she is wildly in love with you, though I do not know why. You can be terribly difficult to live with."

Darcy flushed and looked to the ground, then back to his cousin with a smile. "Forgive me, Fitz, you are correct, of course. My apologies for haranguing you."

"You are forgiven, *Fitz*."

Darcy winced and closed his eyes, taking a deep breath.

"Do you really hate being called 'Fitz' so very much?" the colonel asked.

"I do, though Elizabeth calls me Fitzwilliam now, and I like it much more than I thought I would."

Fitzwilliam gave him a knowing smile. "That is likely why she asked me to call her Elizabeth."

Darcy looked at him in incomprehension.

"Marriage has dulled your wits, Cousin. If she calls you Fitzwilliam, particularly when you are alone, can you not see why she would not wish to address me in the same manner?"

Darcy hardly thought it would be in the same manner, low and sweet and lingering ever so slightly on the second syllable, but he took his cousin's point.

"You are correct, of course. I hadn't thought…"

"You may call me Fitz, if it makes things any easier."

"You do not hate it?" Darcy asked in surprise.

"No, I never have, but you hated it so much I couldn't resist the opportunity to tease you."

Darcy rolled his eyes and Fitz laughed cheerily.

"It is settled: I will be Fitz and you will be Darcy, and Elizabeth shall call you Fitzwilliam, or darling, or sweet dumpling, or whatever she likes, and I will be Richard to her. Are we in agreement?"

Darcy sighed and pursed his lips, then held out his hand to his cousin. "We are in agreement. *Fitz.*"

Colonel Fitzwilliam laughed too loudly for the joke. But then, he always did. "Now go find your wife. I am desperate for a bath."

Elizabeth went over the day's events in her mind as she prepared for bed that evening. She thought it had gone rather well, all things considered.

Conversation had been a bit forced at tea, but not overly awkward, and her new family clearly had great affection for her husband and Georgiana, though they were more formal with him than they were with his sister. Dinner was more of the same, though Elizabeth thought the earl was warming to her. His wife still looked at her as if she were a specimen under glass speared on a pin to be studied, but she was not hostile, nor were her questions intrusive.

The viscount and his lady were harder to read. Lord Lisle had said little at dinner and even less after. His wife had been all that was polite, but she was not particularly warm. She was quite the fine lady, and Elizabeth imagined she thought the new Mrs. Darcy to be a country upstart rising above her sphere.

But Mrs. Darcy could not care overly much. Soon enough, they would see how happy she and her husband were together, and Georgiana as well. That would have to be enough.

The evening after their visitors arrived, Elizabeth was hosting a dinner. So far, she had only entertained the vicar and his family and a neighbor with whom Darcy was particularly friendly. Those dinners had been small and intimate, with simple menus and friendly faces.

Now she had invited four neighboring families and ordered a five-course meal. Rooms had been prepared in the event they were required, and Elizabeth was wearing a new gown. Georgiana was nervous, flitting from window to chair and back again, waiting for their guests to arrive.

"Do sit down, dearest. They will be here soon enough," Richard chided gently.

Darcy smiled at his sister from his place near the fire. Elizabeth was off somewhere speaking to Mrs. Reynolds, while the remaining family had not come down for dinner yet.

Darcy was not uneasy exactly. He had great faith in his wife's abilities. It was only dinner. But he did feel the weight of the evening, of how it would set their place amongst the local society and debut his wife as a hostess. This dinner would be talked of, in great detail, and if it went badly, it could take years for opinions to change.

Elizabeth entered the room with a radiant smile. He relaxed at the sight of her. She was brimming with confidence and good cheer.

Soon enough, his Fitzwilliam relations joined them. Lady Lisle was somewhat overdressed and weighed down by jewels but still very pretty. Elizabeth smirked and caught the eye of the colonel, who made such an eloquent expression that she had to bite her lip to keep from laughing. Lord Lisle looked supremely bored but well turned out. His parents were perfectly dressed, perfectly coiffed, and comported themselves perfectly, as expected.

Elizabeth tried not to roll her eyes at how very formal everyone was. Were it not for the good colonel, she might have despaired at ever coming to befriend anyone in her husband's family.

Finally, their guests arrived. The Watsons were an elderly couple who brought with them their eldest son and his wife as well as their rather dashing youngest son, a captain in the navy currently visiting his family. Next were the Beechams, a middle-aged couple with two unattached daughters, Margaret and Julia, the younger only recently out. The Darcys had hopes that Miss Julia and Georgiana would become friends. Sir Edmond and Lady Sarah Ludlow arrived, wreathed in pomp and glory, and finally, Mr. and Mrs. Wheeler, a local landowner with a good-sized estate that bordered Pemberley.

The Wheelers brought with them their only child and heir, Miss Wheeler, a pretty young woman with honey-colored hair and large green eyes. Colonel Fitzwilliam stood a little straighter when she was announced, and Elizabeth stifled a smile. *So, the colonel is not so impervious after all.*

Luckily for Colonel Fitzwilliam (and perhaps less so for Miss Wheeler), that gentleman was seated on the lady's left. He charmed, he flirted, he saw to her every need and would not allow her a word with anybody else. His utter monopoly of her company would have been considered quite rude if the lady had not seemed equally pleased —eventually.

Lord Aldrington sat on one side of Elizabeth and Lord Lisle on the other. The viscount showed no inclination to converse. He replied to her comments with one-word answers or not at all, and eventually Elizabeth gave him up for naught.

The earl was a better dinner partner. He queried her politely on her family and holiday traditions and plans. After she had told him all she thought would be of interest and was searching for another topic, Mrs. Wheeler, seated on his other side, joined the conversation. She was quite happy to regale them both with the changes she was planning for her home the coming spring. Having recently done extensive renovations on his own manor house, the earl was pleased to listen, and Elizabeth was glad to be relieved of the burden of carrying the conversation.

She looked down the table and thought all was proceeding smoothly. Georgiana was engaged in conversation with Miss Julia and her mother. Darcy seemed happy enough with his aunt on one side and Lady Lisle on the other, though the latter had trained her attention on the handsome captain across the table. Sir Edmond Ludlow was conversing agreeably with Mr. Wheeler and Miss Beecham. That poor girl looked horribly bored—Elizabeth would have to see that she was entertained when the ladies withdrew. Lady Ludlow had been quiet before dinner, but she was conversing animatedly with the viscount now. That man looked engaged for the first time since she had met him.

Satisfied, she looked to her husband and caught his eye. He smiled at her slowly, in that way that began at his eyes and ended with his dimples. She felt her cheeks heat and looked away before she did something silly.

Elizabeth was conversing with the earl and Mrs. Wheeler when she chanced a glance to her left. Lady Ludlow's right hand was conspicuously absent, and the viscount's left dropped beneath the tablecloth, followed swiftly by a flush in the lady's cheeks.

Oh, dear.

As THEY PREPARED for bed that night, Elizabeth asked her husband if Richard had recently met Miss Wheeler, or if the night's flirtations were a game of long standing. After bristling at hearing his cousin's name on her lips, he answered her.

"They have known each other some years. She will be coming into her third season this spring. He may offer for her then," he said simply as he shrugged out of his banyan.

"Truly? I had no idea it was so serious!"

"I do not know that it is *serious.*" He sat on the bed now, leaning against the headboard as he waited for his wife.

"What do you mean? Surely, offering a woman marriage is considered serious!" she countered as she climbed into bed and slipped close to her husband.

He tugged the curtains closed. "It is a serious question, of course, but I do not know that their relationship is serious as yet. He is considering her at this point."

"Has he said as much to you?"

"No, I am merely reading the signs."

"And yet you maintain that their relationship is not serious?"

"Elizabeth, not every man is passionately in love when he offers marriage. I daresay the majority of them are not. We are the exception, not the rule, my love."

He kissed her forehead and pressed her shoulder so she would roll onto her side. He tucked his knees behind hers, and she threaded her feet between his legs. "Your feet are cold."

"And your legs are warm. What a wonderful combination."

He could hear the smile in her voice. "Minx."

"Miser."

"You shall pay for that, madam."

She shrieked as his fingers drove into her ribs. "Stop! Stop! I beg you!" she cried between gales of laughter.

"Never!" He slowed his tickling and pressed his face into her neck. "Do you recant your statement, madam?" He growled and kissed her skin below her jaw, then moved toward her ear.

She let out a breathy sigh. "I do, sir. You are most generous."

He laughed lightly. "I had never thought you would capitulate so easily."

"You think I have capitulated? I thought I had gotten exactly what I wanted." She smirked into the darkness.

His lips stopped their teasing motions, and he froze for a moment. "Minx."

Elizabeth laughed until her lips found a better occupation.

"ELIZABETH, THE WHEELERS' carriage has just pulled into the drive," said Darcy as he entered the conservatory.

"Wonderful! I am happy she is come so early."

"Mrs. Wheeler?"

"No, silly! *Miss* Wheeler. I invited her to spend a few days with us. And the Miss Beechams. Georgiana has been quite lonely this winter, and I am afraid I haven't spent as much time with her as I would like. I thought it would be a good opportunity for her to make friends."

He looked at her skeptically, and she furrowed her brow.

"Do you not approve? I thought you liked the Beechams! You aren't upset I asked them without speaking to you, are you? You did say that I should run the house as I see fit and that I may invite whomever I like. I thought—"

He silenced her with a finger to her lips.

"Elizabeth, I like the Beechams very well, and I am happy you are thinking of Georgiana's comfort. You may invite whom you please, of course; you are mistress in practice as well as name. I am merely surprised, that is all. And I should like to be assured you invited Miss Wheeler here for Georgiana and not for Fitzwilliam." He tilted his chin down and looked up at her in that way he did when he was trying to divine her motives.

She smiled winsomely. "Of course I invited her for Georgiana. I wanted to invite Miss Julia, they got on so well at dinner the other day, and I could hardly invite her without including her elder sister, but Miss Beecham would be in the way of the younger girls and possibly lonely herself. And I did not want her to think I had invited her for the colonel, so I included Miss Wheeler."

"I see. The elder two will occupy each other so that Georgiana may grow closer to Miss Julia. And with three young women here, no one will think they were singled out for my cousin. A wonderful plan, my dear." He nodded in approval and bowed, turning to leave the room.

Elizabeth returned her attention to the greenery she had been arranging, placing a bright red holly stem just so. "Thank you. And if Miss Wheeler happens to spend a little time with the colonel, and they happen to come closer to an understanding, we will have done them a kindness."

Darcy stopped and turned around slowly until he was facing his wife's back. "Elizabeth" —he drew her name out—"what are you planning?"

"Nothing, my love! Nothing at all. I am merely giving our sister an opportunity to make friends while also giving our cousin the chance to know a lady better. It is hardly devious." She stabbed the last stem into the arrangement and turned to face him, lowering her shears.

He almost stepped back involuntarily but stopped himself a moment before he moved. "Very well, my dear. I shall trust your judgment."

She nodded in thanks and he left the room, wondering if he had just been outmaneuvered.

THAT EVENING, Richard tried to find a moment to speak with Miss Wheeler, but Georgiana kept her friends close.

He was standing on his own when Elizabeth approached him and said, "You will not succeed like that, Richard."

"Oh? And how will I succeed?"

She nearly sighed. "Really? You can march against Napoleon, but you cannot find a way to talk to a lady in your cousin's home? I fear for England!" She smiled and walked away, leaving Colonel Fitzwilliam both frustrated and amused.

Determined, he strolled over to where Miss Wheeler was sitting with the Miss Beechams and Georgiana. He struck up a conversation with the group but, soon enough, the elder Miss Beecham had monopolized his attention and Miss Wheeler had gone off to get a cup of tea.

He caught Elizabeth's eye across the room and sent her a pleading look. She looked heavenward but then nodded, causing the colonel to briefly place his hand over his heart in thanks.

Elizabeth ended her conversation with Lady Aldrington and made her way to the tea table, where Miss Wheeler was standing with Miss Julia just as the latter was leaving.

"Are you enjoying the evening, Miss Wheeler?" she asked.

"Oh, yes! Very much so. Thank you for inviting me. It was very kind of you."

"Thank you for coming! You are one of our nearest neighbors. I should like to know you better."

Miss Wheeler smiled genuinely. "I should like that as well, Mrs. Darcy. Tell me, is Derbyshire much different from where you lived before? I heard you are from the South, but I do not know where."

"My father's estate is in Hertfordshire, and yes, it is quite different."

And so they began. They spoke of landscapes and travel, of music and books, the theater and opera, and which plays they favored. After half an hour, Elizabeth realized she had monopolized their guest and had not led the young woman to Richard at all.

Colonel Fitzwilliam caught up with Elizabeth as she ascended the stairs on her husband's arm.

"A fine lieutenant you are!" he whispered in her ear as he walked beside her.

"Why are you whispering to my wife, Fitz?"

"He is disappointed at my performance in a mutual endeavor," she said to her husband.

She turned back to Richard. "All is not lost, Cousin. I did obtain some useful information, and she is here for three more days. We may try again tomorrow."

He sighed and nodded, then turned toward the guest wing as Darcy glared at his retreating back.

As soon as the door was closed on their room, he faced his wife with a stern expression. "What are you and my cousin up to?"

"Nothing terrible, my dear, and he is my cousin, as well. Or have you already forgotten that what's yours is now also mine?" She placed her hands on his arms where they were crossed over his chest and smiled sweetly. "Do not be cross with me, love. I am only being practical." She stretched up and kissed his chin, then disappeared behind the door to her dressing room.

She was back ten minutes later in a long nightgown and velvet robe. He was sitting on the bed in his banyan with a curious look on his face.

"What are you thinking of?" She blew out the lone candle and climbed in beside him. She waited patiently for him to begin speaking.

"What do you mean when you say you are being practical?"

"Ah. Well, the colonel is your nearest relation and a close friend." Darcy nodded. "I assumed you cared for his happiness."

"I do."

"And I am quite fond of him myself." She felt her husband stiffen beside her. "I have wanted a brother my whole life, and I feel quite lucky to finally have one. I know he is not a brother exactly, but a cousin is close enough and—"

She could not finish her statement because her husband quickly grabbed her and pulled her beneath the covers with him, smothering her with kisses.

She laughed and cried, "Fitzwilliam! What has come over you?"

"I am simply glad to be the only man in your affections, my dear, that is all."

She smoothed the hair away from his eyes tenderly. "Did you ever think you were not? Allow me to assure you that you are the only man who has ever touched my heart, and I feel quite certain that you are the only man who ever shall."

"I know that, Lizzy, I do, but sometimes, when I see how alike you and Fitz are, I feel...."

He searched for words and she provided an answer. "Insufficient?"

"Yes. Forgive me, my love. I do not doubt you, not at all."

"You should not. But I do know how you feel." He looked at her quizzically. "When we were in London, and we met all those lovely ladies with accomplishments and titles and dowries, I feared for a moment that you would regret me, that you would wake up five or ten years from now and wish you had married one of them."

"No!"

She placed a finger over his lips.

"But then I realized something. You are Fitzwilliam Darcy of Pemberley. A fine figure of a man with an equally fine estate." She smiled and traced her finger over his nose and cheekbones. "And you are no young pup. If you had wanted one of those ladies, you would have chosen one by now. Nothing stood in your way. They might be more similar to you in breeding and situation, and even in temperament, but it is precisely our differences that make us so perfect for one another. Once I realized that, well, all my fears melted away."

He kissed her softly and rested his forehead against hers. "Perfect for each other, are we?"

"Absolutely." She kissed him quickly. "And it is because of my very great happiness with you that I wish all my family to have the same. I wish it for my sisters Kitty and Mary, and for Georgiana, and for the colonel. Such happiness should be known by more than the two of us."

The room was dim, lit only by the fire, but she could see his eyes glowing as he looked at her. She was coming to understand that look. He was proud of her and proud to have her.

"And you call this being practical?" he teased.

"It is practical in this instance. The Wheelers are one of our closest neighbors and Miss Wheeler is their only child. Whomever she marries will be our neighbor for many years to come. You will have to conduct business and discuss estate matters with him. A bad choice would be irritating at best and disastrous at worst.

"Besides all that, I rather like her. I would like to make a friend of her, and it would be nice to have a female friend nearby. After all, one day Georgiana will leave Pemberley. I must diversify my circle."

He laughed quietly. "You are quite the clever little minx, do you know that?"

"Thank you," she said proudly.

"So you will help Fitz secure Miss Wheeler?"

"If that is what they both want, then yes. At the moment, I am simply trying to help him speak to her." She propped herself up on her elbow. "You could help."

"Me?"

"Yes, you! Another person to assist would be marvelous."

"I do not know. I feel odd interfering in Fitz's affairs."

She gave him an incredulous look.

"He is a grown man! He has been to war. He does not need our help."

Elizabeth huffed. "If he does not need our help, then why did he not speak more than five words to Miss Wheeler tonight?"

"Fitz is very resourceful. I am certain he will think of something."

UNWILLING TO LEAVE matters to chance, Elizabeth rose early and sent off a note to her cousin and another to Miss Wheeler. She was in the entryway long before breakfast, dressed in the riding habit her husband had insisted she order but that she had never actually worn, as riding was rather far down her list of enjoyable activities.

Soon enough, the colonel joined her. "I'm surprised you wished to ride out with me. I thought you disliked it."

"Oh, it has its uses."

"Why do I have a feeling you are up to something?"

"Fear not, Cousin. Everything I do is to your benefit."

She looked towards the stairs and smiled. "Ah, Miss Wheeler! What a fetching habit! I do love that color."

"Thank you, Mrs. Darcy. Yours is very nice as well."

Elizabeth brushed a hand down her navy riding clothes. "Thank you. I rather like the color. If only I could wear something so dark outside of riding!"

They exchanged pleasantries, and finally Elizabeth said, "Miss Wheeler, the colonel and I have a dispute of sorts. Perhaps you could settle it for us."

"I would be happy to assist."

"Colonel Fitzwilliam was telling me that there is a grove of willow trees on the far side of the estate near the border to Walnut Grove, but I have never seen it. Tell me, do you know if such a grove exists?"

Miss Wheeler looked thoughtful for a moment. Before she could answer, Elizabeth spoke again. "I know! Let us ride in that direction and we will see for ourselves."

"That is a splendid idea," agreed Miss Wheeler. "From the fence between the pastures, you may see the folly I was telling you of yesterday."

"Perfect!"

Colonel Fitzwilliam was beginning to see the merit in his cousin's plan and stood by smiling, waiting for an opportunity to offer himself as escort.

"Are you going to join us, Colonel?" asked Miss Wheeler.

Both Elizabeth and Richard were pleasantly surprised by her boldness.

"I believe I shall, thank you."

They were gathering their gloves and hats when Mrs. Reynolds entered and asked to see Mrs. Darcy. Elizabeth conferred with her near the door for a moment, then returned to her guests.

"I am sorry, but I won't be able to join you this morning. Something has come up which requires my attention. But please, do go and enjoy your ride. Richard, I depend on you to tell me if this folly of Miss Wheeler's is worth my riding all the way out there," she said with a smile.

Neither of her companions seemed too disappointed by her defection and, just as they were walking out the door, Richard turned and mouthed "thank you" to Elizabeth. She winked in return and went off to change. *Not require any assistance, indeed.*

AT TEA THAT AFTERNOON, Richard and Miss Wheeler sat near each other and spoke at length, largely because Elizabeth had encouraged Miss Darcy to play a duet with Miss Julia and had requested that Miss Beecham turn their pages. Elizabeth sat with Lady Lisle, who said nothing at all, and Lady Aldrington, who had a great deal to say on topics of meagre interest.

Mr. Darcy, the lucky man, was playing billiards with the viscount and earl. Thus they were happily situated when Captain Watson was announced. Georgiana hit a wrong note and then quit playing altogether, while Lady Lisle flushed quite prettily.

Elizabeth raised a brow and rose to greet their visitor.

"My husband and the earl are at billiards, if you would prefer to be taken to them," she offered.

"That is not necessary. I am happy to visit with the ladies," he said with a charming smile, which he turned on the entire room.

Elizabeth was immediately uneasy. She no longer trusted men who charmed one and all indiscriminately. She had once thought the colonel such a man but, upon closer acquaintance, he was more amiable than charming with strangers and only truly charming with those he knew. This captain reminded her entirely too much of Mr. Wickham, and Georgiana's apparent susceptibility to such men worried her more than she liked.

She led the newcomer to a seat near hers and offered him tea. Before she could hand him his cup, Lady Lisle had prepared a plate of sweetmeats and little cakes and presented it with a smile that could only be called catlike.

Elizabeth wondered at it and whether the looks between the two of them meant what she thought they meant. If they did, was Lady Lisle really brazen enough to behave so in front of her mother-in-law? In her cousin's home?

Unfortunately, Elizabeth did not know the lady well enough to say one way or the other. She only knew it was becoming decidedly uncomfortable sitting between the two of them.

Georgiana and Miss Julia finished their duet and joined the others. With a burst of confidence, Georgiana took the nearest seat to the captain and smiled, which he returned cordially, though with no interest.

To Elizabeth's relief, her sister's courage did not extend to talking to him. Miss Julia sat near her friend and seemed disinterested in any of the goings on around her. Miss Beecham sat next to Miss Wheeler, dividing her time between Colonel Fitzwilliam, who was too much the gentleman to allow his irritation at her interference to show, and Mrs. Darcy, who was rapidly trying to discern the meaning of the looks passed between all the different parties in her drawing room. Lady Aldrington seemed oblivious to it all, and Elizabeth could not help but wonder if she was being purposely obtuse, or if she genuinely did not realize what was happening.

The dinner hour was fast approaching, and Elizabeth felt she had no choice but to invite the captain to stay for dinner. He accepted readily; Lady Lisle gave him a bright smile. Georgiana blushed and looked at the carpet.

Elizabeth rolled her eyes when no one was watching.

HER MAID WAS PUTTING the finishing touches on her hair when her husband appeared in the dressing room door, looking impeccable as always, leaning easily against the doorframe.

Elizabeth dismissed her maid and turned to face her husband.

"You look lovely," he said.

"You look very handsome."

"Well, aren't we a well-matched pair?"

She smiled, then remembered what she had to tell him. "I think Lady Lisle is interested in Captain Watson."

"Interested?"

"Yes. She flirted with him quite openly at tea, and he was more than happy to see her."

"That does not surprise me. She has always preferred men in uniforms."

"Fitzwilliam!"

"'Tis true. She flirted with Fitz years ago, but he would not cuckold his own brother."

Elizabeth's eyes grew round. "Truly? Do you think she would go so far in someone else's house?"

"'Tis easier than in her own house," he mumbled. "I must tell you something. Lisle informed me only an hour ago that he ran into Sir Edmond Ludlow on his ride this afternoon and invited him to dinner."

"Your cousin invited Sir Edmond to dinner at our house?" Darcy nodded.

"Without mentioning it to you until an hour ago?" He nodded again.

"Is he always so presumptuous?"

"Yes."

"Oh, dear. Have you told Mrs. Reynolds? Cook will not be happy."

"I informed Turner. He will ensure all is ready. There is something else I must tell you."

"What is it?"

Darcy rubbed his hand across the back of his neck and paced a few steps away, then returned.

"Come," said Elizabeth. She led him out of the dressing room and into the bedchamber, where he had more room to pace. She sat on the chair by the fireplace, watching her husband walk to the window and back twice before he began.

"It is not something I enjoy speaking of, and certainly not anything a man wishes to discuss with his wife of only a month."

"A month and five days," she corrected.

He could not help but smile at that and, for a moment, he stopped his pacing and merely looked at her, an odd light in his eyes.

"Very well, my wife of five weeks, I will come out with it. Before his marriage, Lord Lisle had an ongoing affair with Mrs. Baker, a young widow. It went on for some time until they both married others, and I am not entirely certain it stopped even then."

At Elizabeth's look of confusion, he clarified, "Mrs. Baker is now Lady Ludlow."

Elizabeth's mouth dropped open, and she could not speak for a full minute.

"Do you suppose they are trying to carry on an, an...assignation here? Or that they already are?"

"I would not put it past my cousin to try, though I cannot say for certain of the lady. He was gone riding for some hours this afternoon, and I do not believe for a moment that he ran into Sir Edmond in Lambton. What would either of them have been doing there?"

"You think he met Lady Ludlow—by design?"

Darcy nodded.

"And then, unable to part with her, he invited her and her husband for dinner and told you he had stumbled upon the husband?"

"That sums it up neatly."

Elizabeth took a deep breath. "I confess I do not know what to do with this information. I had thought hosting your family would bring challenges, but this…"

"I know," Darcy said somberly.

"Well, dinner must be shortened. I will speak with Mrs. Reynolds about eliminating one of the courses. Dessert will be served in the drawing room, and I will lead the ladies out early. Can you ensure the men return quickly? That will hopefully stave off anyone hoping for an invitation to stay the night."

"Yes, of course. Well thought, my dear," he said with a sad smile.

Before they left the room, she grabbed his hand and squeezed. "I am sorry, Fitzwilliam."

"Whatever for?"

"That you are facing this situation at all. I know how you despise deceit."

He kissed her forehead and took a deep breath, then squared his shoulders. "You are correct, but it must be dealt with. Pemberley is my home, not Lisle's. I will not see it turned into a den of iniquity."

Elizabeth stifled a smile. Her husband could be rather dramatic when the mood struck him.

"Once more unto the breach."

DINNER WAS a cross between a disaster and a comedy of errors.

Miss Wheeler was placed next to Colonel Fitzwilliam, which seemed to please them both. They were the few happy diners.

The rest of the guests filed into the dining room and proceeded to sit wherever they liked. Lady Lisle blatantly ignored the seating cards, sitting next to Captain Watson. Lord Lisle escorted Lady Ludlow to her chair and took the one beside her that was meant for his father. Georgiana, finally sensing that something was very off, sat between the colonel and Miss Julia.

Elizabeth smiled and signaled for the first course to be served, planning to rush through the meal as fast as possible without being conspicuous.

The first course was uneventful, though Georgiana and Miss Julia continually darted furtive looks around the table, then back to each other. Colonel Fitzwilliam eventually looked away from Miss Wheeler long enough to notice Darcy's stern demeanor, Elizabeth's discomfort, and his brother's Cheshire grin. He met Darcy's eye, but his cousin only shook his head. When he looked to Elizabeth, she sent him a quick look of exasperation, followed quickly by a false smile for the earl at her side.

Across the table, it was clear Lady Lisle was engaging in some form of flirtation under the tablecloth. Her hands were busy cutting her food, but her countenance was entirely too pleased and her posture strained in the manner of someone whose legs are outstretched. Captain Watson, on her left, was flushed and beginning to sweat near his temples, though the room was barely warm.

Finally, after three courses (the last pitifully thin at Elizabeth's direction), Mrs. Darcy rose and asked the ladies to follow her. As soon as they entered the drawing room, she had the footman open the doors to the music room and asked Julia and Georgiana to play for them. Miss Beecham agreed to sing, thankfully, and Elizabeth felt she had at least protected the youngest members of their party from the goings on.

She instructed a servant to have their guests' carriages ready to depart within the hour, no later, and made a study of the sky, happy to see there were no rain clouds in sight.

Quite to her surprise, Lady Aldrington claimed a headache and retired early. Perhaps she saw more than Elizabeth gave her credit for and simply did not wish to witness her son's mischief.

Elizabeth looked around at the holly-draped mantle, the garlands over the doors, and the similarly adorned banisters in the hall. She had spent such time decorating, wanting to make everything magical and as perfect as possible. But her husband's family seemed impervious to her holiday efforts.

And to think she had been ashamed of *her* family's behavior!

When the gentlemen rejoined the ladies, the earl immediately went upstairs to see to his wife. Unsurprisingly, Lord Lisle went straight to Lady Ludlow. Darcy met Elizabeth's eye and followed his cousin, intent on interrupting whatever they were planning. Lady Lisle was hovering near the kissing bough hung in the doorway, clearly awaiting someone.

The next hour was a busy haze. Captain Watson tried to kiss Lady Lisle under the mistletoe but, just as he was leaning in, Colonel Fitzwilliam elbowed him out of the way and kissed his sister on the temple. She looked quite put out, but the colonel was unrepentant.

Miss Wheeler was not happy to see the man who had been pursuing her relentlessly kissing another woman, but she quickly realized something was afoot and acted as a sort of second to keep Captain Watson and Lady Lisle apart.

In all the confusion, Miss Beecham had positioned herself in just the right place to be kissed by both the colonel and the captain, which made Georgiana flush horribly and Miss Wheeler look at her old neighbor with daggers in her eyes.

Within a half hour, Colonel Fitzwilliam had kissed every woman in the room, including Elizabeth…though that was by accident, as she had been stopped near the kissing bough by a distraught Georgiana (upset because the dashing captain had kissed three ladies and not one of them had been herself), and Colonel Fitzwilliam had wanted to comfort his ward. Miss Julia called out that they were under the kissing bough, and he had looked up to see several berries on the mistletoe. He carefully plucked one, handed it to Elizabeth, and kissed her on the forehead. Miss Julia clapped, and Georgiana laughed, finding it hilariously funny for some reason.

The awkward kiss did serve the purpose of drawing Darcy away from Lord Lisle and his paramour. But all he got for his trouble was a kiss from Miss Beecham and another from a reluctant Miss Wheeler, which caused Fitz to glare at him for a change. Darcy could not help but smirk in response and bowed rather prettily to Miss Wheeler, while his wife shook with laughter.

By the time Miss Wheeler said she was tired and would retire, dragging the Miss Beechams and Georgiana with her, Lord Lisle was glaring at Darcy for interfering in his fun, and Lady Lisle attempted to escape the room unnoticed no fewer than three times before being thwarted by Elizabeth, who would call her back and ask her opinion on something.

Finally, the guests left and the party retired upstairs, but not before an unexpected invitation was given and accepted.

As SOON AS she entered her room, Elizabeth removed her jewels and gown and fell across the bed in sheer exhaustion. Her husband soon joined her.

"Thank god that is over," said Darcy as he collapsed onto the bed and draped one arm over his face.

"I cannot believe your cousins are going to Oakwood." Oakwood was Sir Edmond Ludlow's estate, five miles north of Pemberley.

"I cannot believe they were invited!"

"Do you suppose Sir Edmond knows about his wife and Lord Lisle?"

"Of course he knows!"

"Then why?" she trailed off, perplexed.

"My dear, other people's marriages are not our problem, thankfully, or our concern. Lisle has his heir and doesn't seem to care what his wife does. Ludlow has two sons at Cambridge and seems equally unconcerned about his wife's behavior. If that is how they choose to live, so be it." He sighed and rubbed his tired eyes. "As long as they are not here."

"But Lady Lisle agreed to go! She was nearly ecstatic at the invitation." Elizabeth shook her head. "I do not understand how she can happily watch her husband seduce another woman."

"I do not think she intends to watch him. Oakwood borders the Watson estate. She will likely spend her time with the good captain."

"*That* explains why he seemed so happy," Elizabeth grumbled. "They aren't even staying for Christmas!"

"Did you wish them to?"

"Not truly. But it does seem rude to accept a Christmas invitation, then not stay for Christmas."

"I hate to say it, love, but they likely accepted because of our neighbors, not us."

"Oh, of course you are right. I feel rather stupid for not thinking of it myself." She sighed and rolled onto her side to face her husband. "That certainly explains why Lady Lisle had no interest whatsoever in talking to me. I had wondered why she bothered coming if she disliked me so. I had thought the earl forced them, or perhaps it was for appearances."

"That may have played into it, but I do not think they would do anything they didn't truly wish to do."

He traced his fingers over Elizabeth's arm slowly, his eyes drifting closed.

"The look on your face when Lord Lisle asked if you minded if they left tomorrow!" Elizabeth laughed. "I thought you would pack his trunks yourself!"

"I was tempted," he grumbled.

"At least Richard has made progress with Miss Wheeler. She seems to be growing quite attached to him."

"Mmhmm."

"The more I know her, the more I like her."

He grunted.

She smiled at how he had fallen asleep without even getting under the coverlet. She tugged his arm and pulled him until she had tucked him mostly under the covers, then pulled the blankets up over them both. She nestled into his side, her head on his chest, and kissed him sleepily.

"Goodnight, Fitzwilliam."

"Goodnight, dearest. Lizzy?"

"Hmm?"

"Next year, let's do Christmas with your family."

ELIZABETH ADAMS IS A BOOK-LOVING, tango-dancing, Austen enthusiast. She loves old houses and thinks birthdays should be celebrated with trips—as should most occasions. She can often be found by a sunny window with a cup of hot tea and a book in her hand. She writes romantic comedy and comedic drama in both historical and modern settings. She is the author of *The Houseguest, Unwilling, On Equal Ground, The 26th of November,* and *Meryton Vignettes: Tales of Pride and Prejudice,* and the modern comedy *Green Card.* You can find more information, short stories, and outtakes at ElizabethAdamsWrites.-wordpress.com.

ACKNOWLEDGMENTS

Give us a thankful sense of the blessings in which we live, of the many comforts of our lot, that we may not deserve to lose them by discontent or indifference.
—Jane Austen

I am forever grateful for the talented authors who have joined me on this journey into the Wild West that is now modern-day publishing, and thankful for the peer groups, bloggers, and readers who have encouraged and supported indie projects.

In the spring of 2017, I had the good fortune to visit Chawton House, as well as the Cottage. The day left a lasting impression on me. I look forward to the day when I return. This collection of Christmas stories was an inspired idea after the publication of the anthology *Rational Creatures*, October 2018. In a mad flurry, the following have donated their time and creativity to produce this collection in hopes that all the proceeds might help in the continuation of good at the Great House, ensuring the work of women writers will continue to be discovered and treasured long into the future. Thank you authors Elizabeth Adams, J. Marie Croft, Amy D'Orazio, Lona Manning, Anngela Schroeder, Joana Starnes, and Caitlin Williams for writing *Pride and Prejudice* stories on-demand. Thank you, Debbie Brown, for proofing. Much gratitude to author Karen M Cox for graciously formatting this collection as well. The cover is my own DIY design and I beg your forgiveness for any errors. I hope you enjoyed this collection in the same affectionate spirit it was created. Your positive reviews at Amazon will surely encourage others to buy the collection. Thank you for supporting this effort and Chawton Great House.

CHRISTINA BOYD wears many hats as she is an editor under her own banner, The Quill Ink, a contributor to Austenprose, and a commercial ceramicist. A life member of Jane Austen Society of North America, Christina lives in the wilds of the Pacific Northwest with her dear Mr. B, two busy teenagers, and a retriever named BiBi. Visiting Jane Austen's England was made possible by actor Henry Cavill when she won the Omaze experience to meet him in the spring of 2017 on the London Eye. True story. You can Google it.

If you liked *Yuletide,* you might like *The Darcy Monologues, Dangerous to Know: Jane Austen's Rakes & Gentlemen Rogues,* and *Rational Creatures.*

Manufactured by Amazon.ca
Bolton, ON

10314617R00111